NONPROFIT

A NOVEL

MATT BURRIESCI

New Issues Poetry & Prose

Western Michigan University
Kalamazoo, Michigan 49008

First American Edition, 2015.

ISBN-13: 978-1-936970-29-2

Library of Congress Cataloging-in-Publication Data:
Burriesci, Matt
Nonprofit: A Novel/Matt Burriesci
Library of Congress Control Number: 2013949849

Editor: William Olsen
Managing Editor: Kimberly Kolbe
Layout Editor: McKenzie Lynn Tozan
Copy Editor: Sarah Kidd
Art Direction: Nick Kuder
Cover Design: Aaron Cooper
Production Manager: Paul Sizer
The Design Center, Gwen Frostic School of Art
College of Fine Arts, Western Michigan University

This book is the winner of the Association of Writers & Writing Programs (AWP) Award for the Novel. AWP is a national, nonprofit organization dedicated to serving American letters, writers, and programs of writing.

Go to www.awpwriter.org for more information.

NONPROFIT

A NOVEL

MATT BURRIESCI

NEW ISSUES

 WESTERN MICHIGAN UNIVERSITY

Also by Matt Burriesci:
Dead White Guys: A Father, His Daughter, and the Great Books of the Western World

For Erin Kemper

Make upon it as many grave allegories and glosses as you will, and dote upon it you and the rest of the world for as long as you please: for my part, I can conceive no other meaning in it, but a description of a set at tennis in dark and obscure terms.

—François Rabelais,
Gargantua

RADISHES

One time in Chicago, a cow kicked over a lantern and burned the city to the ground. This was a positive development. Narrow, twisted, dirty corridors laid for horses now gave way to broad boulevards and electrical grids designed on clean Cartesian logic. Combustion, communication, and sewage could suddenly be accommodated. The only way the city could become modern was to destroy it and begin again from scratch.

You think the District of Columbia could use a good fire as your GPS lies to you and tells you to turn left when there is no left. Designed by a cruel Frenchman when the horse-drawn buggy was cutting-edge, the city is laid out on a series of intersecting wagon wheels; traffic circles serve as hubs for spokes that radiate out to other traffic circles. It's hard to orient yourself. Everything is diagonal and circular. Streets end abruptly only to resume under different names blocks later. Important avenues are constantly blocked for dignitaries or closed for repairs that never cease. One-ways and dead-ends abound. Everything is always being patched. Nothing is ever being fixed. Every so often, the manholes in Georgetown simply explode from a buildup of methane in the arcane sewers.

To get across town at 5:00 on a weekday afternoon is nearly impossible, but you must arrive at the home of Alice Cavanaugh-Williams promptly at 6:00. Back in Chicago, even in the worst traffic, you could travel thirty miles in an hour. But you're quickly learning that everything in DC takes longer to accomplish. You make your way around another traffic circle. The clock strikes 4:55. You haven't yet changed it from Chicago time. You keep adding the hour in your head.

"Just park in the turnaround," her assistant informed you. "It's right by the Vice President's residence. You can't miss it."

Well, she's right about that! The home of Alice Cavanaugh-Williams is a former embassy, an old Georgian brick mansion of four or five stories. You can't quite tell how many as you pull into the semi-circular driveway. There is a Rolls-Royce in the driveway, along with a bronze statue of William Henry Cavanaugh, Robber Baron, Titan of Industry, father of two United States senators, and one undistinguished carpetbagger representative from the state of New Jersey, who once drunkenly beat his wife so savagely he nearly spent an entire night in jail. You have compiled a dossier on Alice Cavanaugh-Williams, as you have with every board member of Quill & Pad. You know her net worth, the value of her contributions to the Kennedy Center. There's a rehearsal room named after her: The Alice Cavanaugh-Williams Rehearsal Room. Officially, she is not an officer of the board, but you have learned that unlike money, titles seldom matter.

You park your eight-year-old Volkswagen Golf behind the Rolls and adjust your tie in the rear view mirror. You should've worn the blue tie. The red is too aggressive. You should've plucked your nose hairs. You're generally a well-groomed fellow, but you do have an overabundance of hair in the wrong places. Left to their own devices, your eyebrows would stretch across your forehead, giving you a menacing visage, not totally unlike the angry blue eagle from the Muppets. You pluck them regularly to blend in, to appear happy and accommodating. It's amazing the difference a little maintenance makes.

An elderly black man in a white tuxedo answers the door. He looks like he stepped out of 1952.

"May I help you?" he asks.

"Uh, I'm John MacManus. I'm here for a six o'clock with Mrs. Williams?"

"Yes. Mrs. *Cavanaugh-Williams* is expecting you," the servant says, gently correcting you. "Please follow me to the sitting room."

You have been in nice homes in your life, but you have never been in a sitting room before. The room is there for sitting. It is a huge room and white in every possible way. The walls are white. The floor is white. Even the large central fireplace is white. On the mantel rests an ancient, weathered statue of a horse head. You doubt it came from Crate & Barrel. There are two white sofas, a white coffee table, and several white chairs in the sitting room, along with a grand white piano, which sits in front of terrace doors. The terrace doors overlook a backyard of surprising scope. Inside the city there is apparently a forest. There is another fireplace outside on a large, covered brick patio, which is decorated like a living room. It is an actual fireplace, with a chimney about twenty feet high. You have never seen such a fireplace outside before.

"May I take your coat, sir?" the servant asks. "Mrs. Cavanaugh-Williams will be with you in a moment."

"Yes, thank you," you say, handing him your coat. One of the buttons is missing and loose thread hangs from the coat. You sit down on one of the white sofas and leaf through the carefully arranged books on the coffee table. There are coffee table books of the Greek Islands, Tuscany, and Turkey, as well as some decorative editions of ancient Greek texts.

You come highly recommended. Everyone said nice things. It was just the economy, you see, the last four years. Lots of talented people had to be let go. They tried to keep you on as a contract consultant, but it was just business. This is a bad time for the nonprofit sector. Endowments have been hammered in the crash, private foundations have reduced their giving, and corporations are tightening their belts. Wealth has been destroyed. Individual giving has dried up as a result. So it was not a reflection on your performance. Anyone would be lucky to have you. You did a terrific job with the theater's contributed revenue. You grew it substantially during your tenure. It was a much larger organization. Why, you'd really be taking a step down to come here. But it's a step up from being unemployed. Of course you come with the highest recommendation; of course you were absolutely excellent.

And if there were unsaid things, what were they? That in the end others were simply more absolutely excellent? Others were retained when you were let go? Well, these were difficult decisions. Difficult times. It's been hard on everyone. It should not reflect on you in the slightest. But it reflects on you, and more than slightly.

You have come here from Chicago for a fresh start. Your wife has found a teaching job. Someone was on maternity leave, and it was good timing. The stars aligned. You have left your family and your friends behind to become Executive Director of Quill & Pad, a venerable nonprofit devoted to advancing American letters. Alice Cavanaugh-Williams is the largest single donor to Quill & Pad. You are surprised that she was not a member of the search committee. The search committee asked you questions about challenges, about your experience managing nonprofit organizations, about your reading habits, about five steps to successful fundraising. You were prepared and eloquent. You've always been good in interviews. You talked about mission alignment, about expectations, about the importance of strategic planning. You analyzed their tax returns, explained where efficiencies could be implemented. You talked about systems and programs and the public good. You plucked your eyebrows prior to meeting with the committee.

It has now been about eight minutes in the sitting room, and a new servant emerges. A young woman of Hispanic descent enters the room, dressed in a maid's uniform, carrying a huge silver platter. The maid's uniform looks almost like a Halloween costume. You stand up to help her because the platter is so large, but she will not accept your help. She seems startled that you even offered. On the platter there is an enormous bowl of freshly made hummus. You have never seen so much hummus in one place. It is a quantity roughly the volume of a basketball. Surrounding the bowl of hummus there are a dozen radish bulbs, uncut, and apparently unwashed, as if they have just been plucked from a garden, with their huge leafy stems overflowing from the platter.

The servant sets the platter down in front of you.

"Would you care for something to drink, sir?" she asks.

"No, no, thank you," you say.

"Mrs. Cavanaugh-Williams will be with you shortly."

After she exits you realize you have no way of actually consuming this hummus. There is no knife, there are no small plates, and all the radishes are uncut. You are very confused. Are you supposed to eat the radishes whole? How does this work?

You sit back on the couch and text your wife:

"In huge house with radishes."

You browse through the picture books of ancient Mediterranean ruins, one after the next, until you exhaust them. A half-hour has now passed, and you need to pee. Should you pee? What is the proper etiquette in this situation? What if she's suddenly available and you're off urinating? You decide you should hold it, but then fifteen more minutes pass, and now you have to pee. You get up and make your way to the foyer, where the original servant is apparently waiting, afraid you're about to run off with the China.

"May I assist you, sir?"

"Uh, yeah, I just need to use the restroom?"

"Very good. It's just this way." He leads you to a door in the foyer and smiles. "Mrs. Cavanaugh-Williams will be with you in a moment."

"Thanks," you say, and you enter the bathroom. There is no toilet visible. In front of you there is an elaborate pedestal sink and cloth towels. Above the sink, where the mirror should be, there is a painting of Franklin Delano Roosevelt. It's a very large painting. It's just Franklin Delano Roosevelt's face, in a gold-leaf frame, where the mirror should be.

There is also a staircase in the bathroom. You have never been in a bathroom with a staircase. It leaves you momentarily confused and paralyzed. It leads up a full floor to a tiny commode, and you ascend after you recover your bearings. You piss in the second-story commode. Then you walk back downstairs and wash your hands, staring at the photo of Franklin Delano Roosevelt where your face should be reflected. When you are finished, you exit the bathroom, and the servant is waiting for you right outside the door. You almost want to give him a report.

"Mrs. Cavanaugh-Williams will be with you in a moment," he says, and he walks you back to the sitting room.

You have now been waiting three-quarters of an hour, and you're starting to get hungry. Those radishes ain't looking so bad now, but you resist, and you settle back down on the couch. You sigh, pick up the Plato, and get through a good chunk of *Republic* before you hear footsteps descending on a staircase. At some unknown instinct you stand up.

A thin, grey-haired woman in a very understated black dress enters the room. She smiles graciously, and you notice her elegant pearl necklace. She extends a bony hand to you, and you take it over the coffee table. She places her other hand on top of yours.

"Mrs. Cavanaugh-Williams," you say.

"John," she smiles, patting your hand with hers. "We're so lucky to have you on board at Quill & Pad. I'm so glad we got a chance to do this."

She pulls her hand away and walks back up the stairs without another word. The servant immediately brings your coat and escorts you to the door.

PART ONE

BENEFIT

Andrew Jackson made delicious cookies. You learn this at the Ritz Carlton in Washington, DC, after the valet hands you one of Andrew Jackson's cookies.

"Welcome to the Ritz Carlton," the valet says, taking your keys and handing you an oatmeal cookie. "That's Andrew Jackson's recipe, sir!"

You are here for the Benefit. It is not your benefit. You are here to see somebody else's benefit in the venue where your benefit will also take place several months from now. The cookie has cranberries. The Benefit is for some organization that helps teachers. The teachers will speak throughout the course of the evening about the importance of the organization. A group of delightful black children will sing you a song. During the salad there will be a video of delightful black children overcoming great adversity with the help of the organization. Over seared duck, a bed of couscous, and fingerling potatoes, a spotlight will locate various teachers around the room. They will speak about the importance of the organization and their important work on behalf of delightful black children. The teachers are strategically placed throughout the cavernous, elegantly decorated ballroom. You won't listen to them. There are too many of them. They all say the same thing. Tears and commitment and life-changing decisions and what-we-need-now.

It's hard work, but I can't imagine doing anything else.

We can't abandon our children to indifference.

You think the duck is an odd choice. It tastes slimy and lukewarm. Why didn't they serve chicken, or at least provide a vegetarian option? The vegetarian option is always tolerable. But no one here is a vegetarian. Everyone here eats meat, and they have always eaten meat. The room is filled with carnivores.

The teachers are not seated.

Before the benefit there is a reception. There are two receptions. You are given the blue card, which entitles you to the VIP Reception. You are not sure if this is better or worse than the Patron reception. The VIP reception is for Patrons. You are not sure if you are a Sponsor or a Benefactor. You are simply a guest.

The Secretary of Education is there with his *aide de camp*. The Secretary does not wear a suit coat. His sleeves are rolled up. He wants to look like he is working. He is working. The Secretary hates benefits, but he appears at one every two weeks. He is there to talk about the importance of private/public partnerships. He is there to raise money and praise the other side. He is there because one of his boss's bundlers made a gentle suggestion that was not a suggestion.

That bundler is a white-haired, skeletal woman in a metallic dress. She introduces the Secretary in a halting, unrehearsed monotone. The Secretary thanks her and delivers remarks from the podium at the front of the ballroom.

"You know," he says, "I know we disagree on a lot in this town, but this is not a partisan issue. I think we can all agree on education."

Everyone nods.

Education is a partisan issue, and you do not all agree.

At the VIP reception you are served Beef Wellington and Tuna Tartar by short, Hispanic men in black vests and bow ties, who smile at you and hand you napkins imprinted with the organization's logo and compelling statistics about education in inner cities.

51% of inner city children read below grade average.

47% come from single parent households.

You can make a difference.

The VIP reception is a sea of white men in striped blue shirts and yellow ties, with strong jaws, emerging jowls, and steely, New England blue eyes. There is no other blue on Earth quite like it. They all look like what you imagine Robert Frost must've looked like. They have homes on the Vineyard. You have never seen them at your Starbucks, your Safeways, or your Shell stations. These institutions do not exist in their cities. They live in different cities hiding inside your cities, in twisted, alcoved streets radiating from unknown, northwestern thoroughfares. They have people to fetch their groceries and fill their cars with gasoline. They live in secret, stately homes located in secret, stately neighborhoods surrounded by tall gates and trees. They have a deeper understanding of the world than you do. They are there because of their wives, who chair and serve on various committees for various organizations, who attend each other's various benefits. The men are dragged along to do their civic duty. Everyone writes each other checks. This is how it is done.

There are young wives and old wives, and they are all married to older men. The young wives are stunning. There are a surprising number of brunettes. More than you expected. They are dressed in tight black cocktail dresses, their ample white breasts pushed up in elegant displays of décolletage. They have ridden horses on private estates. Their fathers have owned yachts and sailboats, and their fathers have dutifully sent their daughters to Wellesley and Georgetown and Duke.

The older women are dressed in colorful gowns that ride up to the neck. Their hair looks lacquered, almost like a hairpiece on a Lego figurine. Young or old, the women wear enormous jewelry. They have a deeper understanding of the world than you do. They have inherited horses and private estates and yachts. Their fathers' names appear on buildings at Wellesley and Georgetown and Duke.

A photographer takes your picture.

"Can I get your name? It's for *Congressional Quarterly*," the photographer says.

You should promote yourself and get seen.

"I'm nobody," you tell him. "I'm just here on a site visit."

At a buffet table you discover a plate of crackers. They look like Wheat Thins, but they are not Wheat Thins. They are the best fucking crackers you have ever tasted.

Then you see someone who used to be the Vice President of the United States.

*

"How about those teachers; aren't they *fabulous?* Let's give them a hand," a skeleton says from the podium in the ballroom. "Thank you, teachers!" The teachers are identified as if they are zebras.

Forty tables of ten stand and applaud, but the teachers have already departed the ballroom.

Corporations and foundations are thanked. A special thank-you to this year's benefit chair, to the benefit committee, to all the patrons and benefactors and special friends. Join us for dessert in the Grand Foyer.

You study the donor card. You appreciate the way it is laid out. You also like the program. The messaging is clear and well-organized. There are things here to steal for your benefit. You run down the list of donors, focusing on the lower end. The napkins are a special touch, and cheap. You are a student of cheap and special touches.

"Ellen Doray Watson," the woman to the right of you proclaims, offering you her hand.

"John MacManus," you say, shaking her hand. A dangling silver charm bracelet hangs from her wrist. "Quill & Pad."

"That's the literary one, right?"

"Yes. The literary one."

"I heard something about that—who was their ED before—Vivian, Victoria…"

"Vanessa Williams."

"Yes, that's right. Vanessa Williams. Like the singer. What an unfortunate name. What happened to her?"

"I don't think there was anything strange," you shrug, although you suspect otherwise. "She took over as the Development Director for a Foundation—cystic fibrosis, I believe."

"Well, good for her. You must have a tough job of it. With the e-books and all that. You know I just read in the paper this morning that Barnes and Noble is shutting a third of its stores?"

"Yes. It's hard to compete in bricks and mortar anymore."

"After Borders they're all that's left. Unless you count Amazon."

"Well. They count."

"But I mean actual *bookstores*, you know? There's something so nice about a bookstore. We used to have a lovely bookstore in my neighborhood—what was it called?—oh, I forget. It was there for years. Then one day it was gone. But I guess it's hard to make a living at it anymore. I can't remember the last time I was actually in a bookstore. Is that what Quill & Pad does? Bookstores?"

"No, not really, no," you say. "We support independent bookstores but it's not really—we were founded with a grant from Harlan Greer, in the late 1950s."

"The mystery writer?"

"Yes."

"My father *adored* his books."

"Yes, well—he wanted literature to have a prominent place in the nation's capital. So he established Quill & Pad to increase awareness of literature among policymakers."

"How do you do that?"

"We have a lobbyist up on the hill. And we have a number of private book clubs around the city, mostly for politicians. We host a public reading series, and we also work with the schools, to bring in books and authors to the schools."

"And the benefit, of course."

"Yes. And the benefit."

"Well. What did you think about the show tonight?"

"I like the napkins," you shrug.

"Ha! I agree. They do this thing at Alvin Ailey, this dance every year; it's breathtaking."

"I'm sorry. I don't know what that is."

"Alvin Ailey. The dance company?"

You shake your head.

"Well. They do this thing. Tonight, I don't know, all those kids," she shakes her head in a scolding manner. "It's over the top. Too much, too much. I'm with AmeriHopes," she says, because you haven't asked yet. You have no idea what that is.

"And what is AmeriHopes?"

"We raise money for education programs in developing countries," she says, and then, after rummaging in her purse for half a second, she produces a crisp brochure. It is red, white, and blue. There's the American Flag, and a bunch of pale white guys in clean, new camping clothes kneeling in front of a shack somewhere that god hates and has always hated. Individual tickets start at $25,000.

"Our gala begins with a dinner and a dance at an airplane hanger, and at the end of the night, everyone boards a DC9 and we take them to a developing country. This year we're off to Guatemala."

You cannot think of a worse possible way to spend a weekend.

"I know it sounds a little crazy," she says. "But you wouldn't believe what happens once we get them there. Something happens to people. Their eyes open up."

You go back to the brochure. Something cares, something America.

"Is that right?" you say.

"Where are you coming from?"

"Chicago."

"Yes, but *where?*"

"The Empire Theater."

"Oh. I've heard of that. Doing what?"

"I was on the fundraising team," you shrug.

You understand that Ellen Doray Watson is after an invite, after your board, after your donors. If you were smart you would be after an invite, after her board, after her donors. And then you chuckle, weirdly, thinking about sequestering Alice Cavanaugh-Williams on a nine-hour flight aboard a cargo plane and depositing her in a jungle.

You're tired. You're thirty-eight and you're tired. You're more tired than you should be at this age. You're tired of cities, but most of all you're tired of the arts. You wish you had studied physics or pharmacy. You wish you weren't that kid who ran the light booth in high school. You wish you'd never wandered into this mission-driven life without any purpose, this churning scandal mill that will eat you up, too, and spit you out like Vanessa Williams, your reputation destroyed, raising money for some disease.

"Yes, the Empire—that one on Michigan Avenue? Is that the one?"

"That's the one."

"That was quite a story. It was in the *Post* here. Beautiful building," she smiles. "You're new to DC then?"

"Only been here a few months."

"Is this your first benefit?"

"In DC, yes," you say. "We had them in Chicago."

"Yes, but they're not the same, are they?" she says dismissively.

"Well I once saw a hotel ballroom in Chicago," you say. "And we've been known to serve rubber chicken on occasion."

"Oh no, that's not—you're so funny! Listen, I grew up in Cleveland. So believe me, I know what you mean. People in this town would be shocked to find out we had indoor plumbing. They're only vaguely aware that New York's there because of the train. But outside that they tend to lump the rest of the country all together, like it's one giant wasteland. You'd be surprised. It's changed a lot, actually. It didn't used to be like that."

"No?"

"No, I don't know what it is," she says. "Well, you're new to DC—and you're very young; you wouldn't remember."

"I'm older than I look," you assure her. "It's because I'm short."

She laughs, touches your arm. She's an arm-toucher. She likes self-deprecating men. You're self-deprecating because you know women like Ellen Doray Watson like self-deprecating men.

It says you have a sense of humor, and that you can be controlled.

"No, I mean there was a time when people actually *socialized* together. They went to each other's houses. Their kids went to school together. Now nobody lives here anymore. Everybody's here three days out of the week and then back to their districts to raise money. That's what it is, really. All the money. You just need so much of it now."

The benefit chair is back on stage, and she steps to the microphone.

"Would you all please join us for dessert and coffee in the Grand Foyer?"

MOTILITY

You can never have children. This news is delivered to you on a Wednesday by a bald man in a labcoat, who shows you a colorful diagram of the male reproductive system. He points to the testes, healthy and pink, and then up to the thin red tubes and things leading up from the testes.

"So this is what a normal system looks like," he says. Your system does not resemble the normal system. You may want to see a specialist. There is talk of morphology, motility, and count.

"When we say 'count,' what we're referring to is quantity, the number of sperm. When we say 'morphology,' what we mean is the way the sperm is shaped. When we say 'motility,' what we're referring to there is the quality of the sperm, its ability to move and fertilize the egg."

You wonder why they don't use the words number, shape, and quality. But in short, there's not a lot of sperm, what remains is mostly deformed, and the ones that are adequately shaped appear "sluggish."

He explains your chances of conception. This probability is compared to your chances of winning the lottery.

"The good news is that you don't have zero sperm. So we have options."

Your options are discussed. Sperm donors. Adoption. In-vitro fertilization. He hands you a pamphlet: "Living with Male Infertility."

You recognize the print style immediately. It is a standard tri-fold brochure on an eighty-pound gloss stock. They didn't need to spring for the gloss. It's not an image-heavy document. Lots of bullets and question marks.

It can be difficult.

You are not alone.

Liesl squeezes your hand and manages a supportive smile. Prior to this moment Liesl's uterus has been pumped full of radioactive isotopes that glow against a certain scan and grant her the gift of intense menstrual cramps that last two weeks. There have been extractions and tests, probes and analyses.

Your job was to enter a small room and masturbate into a tiny plastic cup. There was a La-Z-Boy in the room, a small television, and a VCR. You were taken aback that in such a state-of-the-art fertility clinic, in which life is chemically engineered at the molecular level, they did not yet possess DVD technology. You would've preferred to supply your own pornography. You played the tape in the VCR. The movie was in Spanish. A sweaty, barrel-chested Mexican with a moustache enjoyed anal sex with a blond woman with enormous breasts. Her ecstasy lasted for minutes as he grunted and thrust behind her. Outside you could hear the nurses chatting, doors closing, machines beeping. Someone was talking about *Mad Men*. Despite all obstacles you managed to climax. At your moment of euphoria you fumbled with the plastic cup, trying to catch every sticky drop.

Did you get any on your khaki pants?

You washed your hands, labeled your specimen, and rang a

doorbell for the nurse to collect your cup. You then stood in the room holding a cup of your sperm for three minutes.

The bald man is still talking. You have a 1:00 p.m. with Quill & Pad's accountant. You are trying to understand what the bald man is telling you. The bald man is using words like *irreversible* and *permanent* and *damage*.

You assumed it would be your wife's problem, because, after all, her machinery is infinitely more complex than yours. You are a rigged slot machine set to pay on every pull. She is a symphony orchestra that only rehearses on Tuesdays. There are just so many chances for something to go wrong on her end.

And yet it is you with your monkey-lever and your bad testes; you with your below-average height and your bad skin; you with every physical, intellectual, and moral defect that is the problem in the world.

It was nothing you did, the bald man assures you. It could not be avoided. It is merely a fundamental problem with the way you came out of the womb. Nature doesn't want anything remotely resembling you. How you're here in the first place is a great big fucking mystery, a cosmic genetic experiment gone horribly awry. A long and great Darwinian struggle has concluded with you, a substandard and defective model ill-equipped for life in our times. Your breed cannot survive the future that is coming. You are scheduled to be phased out to make way for the new models.

"Let's focus on the positives," he says.

DIVERSITY

At 1:00 p.m. the Accountant tells you Quill & Pad is bankrupt.

"You've got about ten months of operating cash," he says.

But certainly there is some mistake. You reviewed their tax documents prior to taking this job. You developed a charming PowerPoint presentation to the search committee based on those tax returns. Those documents detailed the organization's various endowments and accounts, and stated under threat of prosecution that there were seven million dollars in the bank. There are billionaires on your board.

"That's not what it says on the tax returns," you say.

"Yes, well, there seems to be a problem with their tax returns," the Accountant explains.

"What do you mean?"

"They're incorrect."

"How could that be?"

"I really can't advise you on this," the Accountant says, leaning back. "I don't think Baugher & Schulte can represent your organization in this matter. There have been material misstatements by management."

"What misstatements?"

"Look, just…" the Accountant sighs, looks around, as if someone else might be in the room. He's a thin, trim man, about your age. You wonder why you never studied accounting. That would be a good life, staring at spreadsheets all day, reading the tax code, telling suckers that they're bankrupt. "Look, man, you seem like a nice guy. We can't represent you. Off the record?"

"Off the record. Yes, whatever."

"Well, I…look, I've never seen anything like this," he says, sliding several stacks of paper over in your direction. Each stack is binder clipped. These are the tax returns from the previous years, the ones you reviewed before taking the job. The ones that showed positive cash flows and large cash balances. "It seems that they've…well, it looks like they've just misstated their revenues for the past four years."

"You mean they lied."

"I didn't say that. There were material misstatements."

"By how much?"

"Over the last four years?" He sighs, leans back. "Combined? It's several million dollars."

"Define several."

"Six."

"Six million dollars?!" you say, snatching up the tax returns. You look at them and then wonder why you're looking at them. There is no point in spending any more time with these documents. Apparently they are works of fiction. "Are you sure?"

"Oh yes," he says. "Without a doubt."

"But how could they do that?" you ask. "How could you miss that? Shouldn't you have caught that in the audit?"

"Your predecessor didn't do audits," the Accountant said. "You're the first one in five years to request an audit. We just prepared and filed the tax returns before this. But once we started the audit we found it pretty quick. And it wasn't hard to find."

"If they didn't do annual audits, where did these numbers come from?" you say, holding up the tax returns.

"They come from you."

"Me?"

"Well, from the previous Executive, I mean. From Quill & Pad. If we're just preparing tax returns, we rely on the accuracy of the information that comes from management. When there are material misstatements..."

"So we just made up our tax returns? For five years?"

"There were material misstatements."

"You didn't bother to check?"

"We rely on the statements of management..."

"So we just told you numbers and you wrote them down? Nobody checked the actual bank accounts?"

"As I said, when we prepare tax returns, we rely on the statements of management..."

"What's the fucking point of hiring an accounting firm if you just use whatever we give you? You just filled out the forms? Didn't you check any of this? Isn't that what you're paid to do? Check shit out?"

"We state very clearly in our letter of engagement that we are not responsible for misstatements made by management. We're happy to prepare the forms and file properly, but that's the extent of our engagement with Quill & Pad."

Suddenly you understand how the economy collapsed. And then you realize that for several years, Quill & Pad has been falsifying Federal tax returns.

"Wait, so...not only are we broke, but we lied to the IRS?"

"We are not responsible for material misstatements by management," he says.

"We have Federal grants," you say. "The National

Endowment for the Arts, the National Endowment for the Humanities—we have hundreds of thousands of dollars coming in from foundations, from corporations—"

"And it was overstated every year. By a fairly large margin. Actually, it's quite consistent. By about one million, five-hundred thousand each year. Four years, six million dollars. And change."

You sigh. You lean back in your chair and rub your face with your hands. You have been in this job for four weeks. You are the Executive Director. You're in the big chair. Quill & Pad is a venerable organization that has been in existence for more than fifty years. Norman Mailer, Gore Vidal, Eudora Welty, and Flannery O'Connor all graced the stages of your benefits over the years. Quill & Pad is legendary for its literary parties, your soirees with the literati and the power brokers of DC There's some story about a dinner party involving Henry Kissinger and Truman Capote. How could this happen?

"So what...all right," you say, leaning forward. "What is our actual cash position? How much money do we actually have right now?"

"Right now? You have $1.5 million in cash and receivables, and another four hundred thousand in reserve. And then there's about fifty thousand in this small endowment your board member manages."

"So two million."

"Yes. But your outstanding liabilities exceed three million."

"And the liabilities are correct?"

"If anything they're conservative," he whistles. "You're actually losing money on your benefit."

"What?"

"I mean if this number's correct, it looks like you're spending about $1.2 million on your benefit, but you're only generating about $800,000 in revenue."

"Wait—okay, that's crazy, but—just, for the year," you say, pinching the bridge of your nose and wincing. "Let's talk about the year. The next eleven months. We spend three million a year. We make about two million. So at the end of the year, we're short a million."

"Yes," the Accountant says. "It looks like when your predecessor overstated the revenue, she liquidated the organization's cash reserves to make up the difference."

"Right, so...and stop me if I'm wrong...what we did was—we ran up huge deficits, lied about the revenue to make it look like we had balanced budgets, and then just drew down money from the cash reserve, and basically counted that as revenue. Is that right?"

"It appears that way, yes," the Accountant says. "So think of it like your savings account. You basically counted your savings as revenue every year. That's not revenue."

"And then we just never corrected the savings account. We just kept drawing it down, but we acted like we'd never spent the money."

"Correct."

"But we *did* spend that money. It's gone. So on paper, on these statements, which we sent to the Federal government, and to all the foundations and corporations supporting us, it says we have about seven million in the bank. But in reality, we've only got about five hundred thousand."

"Right."

"That's a big difference."

"Yes," the Accountant says. "Yes it is."

"And at the end of the year, we'll be short a million dollars. And in the past, we could get away with that, because we actually had money in the bank to cover the deficits. But now we don't. Even though we say we do."

"Correct. So there are a number of ways to—you can handle this a number of different ways. The actual reporting. But the problem is, once you reach that point, the end of the fiscal year, and there's no money left in the cash reserve..."

"We're fucked."

"Essentially you are fucked."

Now you understand why Vanessa Williams jumped ship.

"So basically we need another million dollars," you say. "I need to raise another million dollars in the next eleven months."

"Well. Unfortunately, it's not that simple," he says, as if finding a million dollars is a simple problem. "Information was knowingly withheld from the IRS. There are penalties for that kind of...I can't...there are fines...your nonprofit status can be revoked."

"What would that mean?"

"Well, a number of things," the Accountant sighs, runs his hand through his hair. "If they really want to make an example out of you, they'll revoke your nonprofit status retroactively. For the last four years. Then they'll tax you like a corporation on the income you received in those years."

"For the last four years? How much would that be?"

"Hard to say...probably 25% a year, at best? Conservatively?"

"That's what..." you say, scribbling down some numbers on an envelope. "That's two million dollars. Or more?"

"Probably more," he says. "There are other issues. You've had Federal grants for the past several years. The government could demand that money back."

"In a lump sum?"

"Yes. Technically. I'm not saying they would, but...they could."

"Well how much is that?"

"I don't know. Over four years? Eight, nine hundred

thousand?"

You laugh. You don't know what else to do. So you laugh.

"That's just a rough estimate," he says, trying to comfort you. "Back of the envelope."

"I just got here," you say, but not to him. "I don't even know how the goddamned fax machine works yet!"

"Well, it all depends on what they want to do," the Accountant says. "There's only so much they can get. Well, out of the corporation at least."

"What do you mean 'out of the corporation?'"

"Well technically, you and the board are officers of the corporation. You have signatory authority. After Sarbanes-Oxley—after Enron, you remember that? They passed a law that allows the government to go after your personal assets. Of the individuals with fiduciary responsibility. Because you're an officer of the corporation."

You stand up and turn to the window. From your window you can see the tippy-top of the White House. At first it awed you and now you don't even notice it.

"What are my options?"

"Mr. MacManus, I can't really advise you on this."

"Do I resign? What do I do? I mean, do I...do I call someone? Who do you call?"

"I...I just really can't advise you on this."

"Well do I see a lawyer?"

"I..."

Your phone rings.

"Hold on a second," you say, picking up the phone. "John MacManus."

"Hold the line for Mrs. Cavanaugh-Williams," a voice on the other end says. You can't tell if it's a man or a woman. There are beeps and cracks, and then suddenly you're connected to Alice

Cavanaugh-Williams, who, from the sound of the connection, appears to be calling from the summit of Mount Kilimanjaro.

"Hello?" you say, holding the receiver close to your right ear, and plugging your left with your finger. "Mrs. Cavanaugh-Williams?"

"John?" She says through the static. It sounds like a hurricane is blowing into the receiver. "I've just...remarkable... poetry."

"Mrs. Cavanaugh-Williams," you say, annoyed that you have to say her whole goddamned name every time. "I'm sorry, I think we have a bad connect—"

"Hector Siffuentes. I want him for the benefit."

"Who?"

"He's *huge* in the Gay Latino poet community...." Then she breaks up for a moment, and when she returns, you only hear the word "...Adonis."

"Adonis, what?"

"...importance of diversity..."

"Mrs. Cavanaugh-Williams..."

"...Geographies...fabulous..."

"Mrs. Cavanaugh-Williams, can I call you back? I think we have a bad connection."

"...must get Hector Siffuentes."

Then she hangs up.

"Is everything all right?" the Accountant asks.

INTERLUDE: THE SECRET BIOGRAPHY OF HECTOR SIFFUENTES

Hector Siffuentes is the author of two poetry collections: *Tijuana Adonis* and *Blue Geographies*. He is known for his experimental style, and especially for poems that lack concern for traditional poetic devices, such as meter, rhyme, and stanzas. *Tijuana Adonis* was his breakthrough book when it won the 1992 Roland R. Wajazinski Prize for Poetry from William Tecumsah Sherman Community College Press. The *New York Times Book Review* wrote this of *Tijuana Adonis*:

"The poems in Tijuana Adonis *are as fresh as warm tortillas... courageous, metrically ambivalent, and fierce, these poems trace the challenges of growing up gay and Latino in America."*

Since the publication of *Tijuana Adonis*, Hector Siffuentes has become a vocal advocate for gay rights, appearing on prominent morning talk shows and news programs. He is in high demand on the lecture circuit.

Hector has pale skin, blue eyes, and blond hair. His appearance challenges pre-conceived notions of what it means to be Latino. This is because he is not Latino. He is Eastern European. He is also not a homosexual, and engages frequently in heterosexual sex. Hector is aware that he is not gay. But he himself is confused about his Latino heritage.

Hector Siffuentes grew up in Hoffman Estates, Illinois, where his father was a successful orthodontist. His mother ran a boutique that sold scented candles and knick-knacks for expensive suburban mantelpieces. The ceramic horses from Holland were disturbingly strong sellers.

Hector had been adopted as a baby from the Ukrainian black market, and the orthodontist had re-named him Hector after the character in the *Iliad*. His father had done so hoping his boy would grow up with the courage and honor embodied in the doomed Trojan.

Unfortunately, no one ever informed Hector that he was adopted, and he grew up believing that he had some form of albinism, on account of his astonishingly fair skin and light hair, traits which were typical in Ukrainian offspring, but somewhat rare in the children of third-generation Peruvian-Americans. His parents had been reluctant to reopen the dubious chapter of his adoption, and nobody ever asked too many questions in Hoffman Estates. People assumed he'd inherited his fair coloring from his mother, who was French Canadian by descent.

Hector's adoptive father Joe had only been to Peru once as a ten-year-old child, back in 1954. There, he had been astonished to find the country lacking in many of the modern amenities he took for granted growing up in post-war Chicago. Hector's grandfather had also never lived in Peru. He'd been born in Fond du Lac, Wisconsin, and he was a veteran of World War II. He'd served as a Marine in the Pacific Campaign, where he'd earned three commendations for bravery at the Battle of Saipan. He raised his son Joe to believe that anything was possible in America, so long as he studied hard and became an Orthodontist.

And so Hector's adoptive father Joe Siffuentes, the marginally Peruvian future orthodontist, had grown up in Schaumburg, Illinois, where he ate lots of hamburgers, bought plenty of rock and roll records, and watched loads of television and movies. As a child he did not dream of one day participating in the noble field of orthodontistry. Instead he dreamt of driving a blue corvette convertible and fucking Brigitte Bardot in the mouth. Jesus Christ, those teeth!

His wife had teeth like Brigitte Bardot. She was French (sort of), and she had huge knockers. Her name was Debbie Garrison, and he'd met her in 1966 at a rather raucous party during his first year of Dental School. They drank Harvey Wallbangers out of coffee mugs and went skinny-dipping in the apartment complex pool.

Debbie enrolled in nursing school, and she enjoyed a brief career as a nurse before opening up her own retail business. This was an excellent decision. She made almost as much selling ceramic bullshit as Joe did in corrective dentistry.

Debbie simply couldn't get pregnant. It was a different time then, and there were very few medical options available. Finally a friend of a friend told Joe about a place where they could get a fresh baby, no questions asked.

"Ten grand, in and out," he whispered. "And you're doin' these kids a favor, Joe, these poor kids, they're stuck in these orphanages in Eastern Europe—they got no future, Joe. They *need* people like you and Debbie."

It had all been as easy as promised, and in 1973, they picked up nine-month-old Hector at a Holiday Inn in Galesburg. Papers were exchanged. Debbie held the baby in her arms the whole way home, crying ecstatically. Joe held back tears himself, and looked over at the baby.

"Hector," he said, and Debbie nodded.

It was a big name to grow into, and the Ukranian foundling failed comprehensively. Although beloved and even spoiled, he lacked his mother's business acumen, his father's work-ethic, and his grandfather's courage. He was a sickly and emotionally troubled boy, which his father suspected traced from his days as a neglected orphan in Ukraine, where he was not given the proper care or nutrition.

Debbie loved Hector as if he were her own baby. But the boy never returned this affection, a fact that privately devastated both parents, but which they never discussed openly. He was slow to walk, slow to speak, slow to everything. He was forced to repeat kindergarten, and in his second stint he bit a boy on the nose so badly that his parents were forced into a rather expensive settlement. After that, the boy started seeing a psychologist.

"And how are you feeling today, Hector?"

Most days, Hector felt a profound sense of isolation—of being different, of being *other than*. He didn't like school, or sports, or much of anything. He felt a great ambivalence toward the world, and he could never understand his place in it. His parents compensated for their son's deficiencies by lavishing him with attention and forcing him into every activity possible. There was computer camp, theater, track, the tuba—nothing caught on. They hired tutors, joined the PTA, and used their status in the community to steer the troubled boy through high school.

College was not optional for Hector, because his adopted parents valued education dearly. They didn't fool themselves. They worried desperately for Hector and warned him that college would be difficult for him. Still, they managed to get him into a fine college in Illinois, where Debbie's sister worked as an admissions counselor. Predictably, Hector struggled in school. He couldn't make any friends, and he simply skipped his classes, drank to excess, and smoked marijuana constantly. To this day, Hector has a profound problem with drugs and alcohol. When he began to fail out the second semester of his sophomore year, his father went to have a stern man-to-man with his adopted son.

"Hector," he'd said, wagging his finger at the teenager. "I think the problem is you've never had to work for anything. So that's it. You're getting a job this summer. I think you'll feel differently about money if you have to earn it for a change."

Hector had no idea how to get a job or keep it, but he finally found work on campus at the Latin American Student Association, LASA. He put up fliers for Latin-themed events around campus, and he became overly-invested in campaigns for student governance, especially after falling in love with Olivia Muñoz, LASA's candidate for Undergraduate Student Council President.

Olivia was a gorgeous Mexican-American with jet-black hair and smooth brown skin. She was a political science major, a straight-A student, a staunch feminist, and almost militant about her Mexican heritage. She was incensed by the way people treated her because of her ethnicity. She was disgusted by the oppression and indignities Mexican-Americans had endured for centuries. She was filled with the righteous indignation of a wealthy twenty-year-old.

"We are not second-class students!" she said at a LASA rally.

Because LASA was the only group that really cared about student government elections, she won the office of President in a landslide. And when the commencement speaker chosen was yet another old white guy, as it had been year after year after year at the university, Olivia spoke out against this amazing injustice on behalf of all the people of Latin America, whose leaders were undoubtedly deeply concerned about the graduation ceremonies of small liberal arts colleges in rural Illinois.

In a letter to the Provost, LASA chairwoman and Incoming Student Council President Olivia Muñoz listed the past ten commencement speakers at the college, who had all been old white dudes, and then posed the following provocative questions:

"Are there no accomplished women? Or even accomplished men of color? What kind of message is this college sending, year after year, when our students only see success in the form of a white man? This student council cannot stand behind the choices of a racist administration."

A commencement boycott was urged, and it was at this point that the college administration became nervous. It was 1992, which was historically a bad year for academics to be called racists. They invited Olivia to submit her suggestions for the keynote speaker. Olivia happily obliged, and submitted the name of an excellent Latina poet, who wound up accepting.

Hector sat through the ceremony in awe, staring at Olivia Muñoz on stage as the poet recited beautiful verse he did not understand. At one point, the poet made a reference to *Venus and Adonis*. Hector did not know the myth, the Shakespearean poem, or the Spanish necessary to decipher the poet's complex verse, but he was vaguely aware that it had something to do with love. And so, as he stared longingly at Olivia Muñoz listening to the musical verse, he thought to himself,

"Olivia Muñoz, you are my Adonis."

Infected with romantic love, he began to scribble his feelings for her on graph paper. She loved poetry, and so he wrote poetry. Since he didn't understand it, he wrote what he did not understand, filling his verse with his vague notions of Greek mythology and Mexican heritage, and inside jokes he was sure Olivia would understand. The poems were all written around the stirring story of the presidential election of Olivia Muñoz, whom he referred to in the work as *El Presidente*.

You stand on the podium, El Presidente
You don't know how I feel about you
I don't practice Santeria
I ain't got no crystal ball
Jose Cuervo silver sunset, and I've given away all your
  campaign buttons
We won the battle, we're fighting the war
My Tijuana Adonis

He wrote thirty pages of poetry, and then put it all into a book and had it bound at the local Kinkos. One night in May, near the end of Olivia Muñoz's triumphant single-term as student council president, Hector consumed five Zimas and presented the book to her, along with a hallmark card saying he loved her. The card was signed, "I LOVE YOU HECTOR."

Olivia, who was drunk herself, didn't know what to say. She was touched. She was also *way* out of Hector's league.

"Hector," she said, kissing him on the cheek. "This is...this is so sweet, it is, but...I..."

"You don't like it," Hector said quickly, truly crushed.

"No, no, it's not the poems. It isn't, they're...they're beautiful, Hector," she lied. Secretly, she and her friends would share numerous chuckles over the poetry of Hector Siffuentes. "Actually, I was going to say you should send it out."

"What do you mean, send it out?"

"There are contests...they have fliers for them up all the time in the English building. Listen, if you send me the file, I'll send it in for you."

And so it was that *Tijuana Adonis* became one of 277 entries for the 1992 Roland R. Wajazinski Prize for Poetry from William Tecumsah Sherman Community College Press. The prize was publication and $1,000.

The judge of the prize was a once-prominent poet, but was now a thrice-divorced raging alcoholic with type-2 diabetes. He was paid $250 to read 277 books of poetry, a duty that he discharged with all the seriousness and care that the financial reward demanded. Essentially he gave the job to a twenty-two-year-old graduate assistant he happened to be fucking, and she selected *Tijuana Adonis* as the winner, believing the book to be about the secret homosexual affair between a campaign aide and a prominent Mexican politician.

"This is gonna make some waves!" she thought.

She was partially correct. Although the general public barely noticed *Tijuana Adonis*, despite the golden sticker with a torch on it that said, "WINNER OF THE 1992 ROLAND R. WAJAZINSKI PRIZE IN POETRY" around the edge, Hector Siffuentes became a sought-after visiting writer at colleges and universities around the country. Hector himself was very surprised by this, but he soon found himself making a pretty decent living hopping from one college to another. And the best part was he didn't really have to *do* anything. All he had to do was be gay and Latino, give fifteen-minute readings from *Tijuana Adonis* at campus bookstores, and occasionally comment on the undergraduate poetry of 18-year old girls with low self-esteem, some of whom could be cajoled into drinking with him. He supplied many of these young girls with drugs and alcohol, which often led to lurid encounters in Ramada Inns and Courtyard Marriotts from coast to coast.

And so it was that Hector Siffuentes had spent the last fifteen years of his life traveling the country, reading from *Tijuana Adonis*, and eventually from his new book, *Blue Geographies*, which was published by GLBT Press in 2001.

It was hailed as a bold experiment in Gay Latino poetry.

PART TWO

SECOND OPINION

"All right, let's have ourselves a look-see," the Urologist says, wheeling over to you on his little stool. You're sitting on the examination table, still in your coat and tie, sans pants. "Go ahead and stand up and drop your boxers for me, please."

You stand up and drop your drawers. You fumble with your shirt-tails and your tie, removing them from your genital area. The Urologist puts two fingers on your right testicle like he's taking its pulse. He cocks his head to one side, nods, and then writes something down on the chart resting in his lap. He's a thin, Indian gentleman about your age. Stacked against the wall behind him there are boxes and boxes of Cialis and Viagra. You should've been a urologist. That would be a good life, handling people's scrotums all day. Dispensing boner medication. You wonder how much money urologists make. More than you do.

"Let's go ahead and try the other side," he says. "You may feel a little pressure."

He takes your left testicle's pulse, cocks his head to the right, and smiles.

"I want you to hear something," he says, wheeling backwards

on his little stool. He grabs a stand with a small machine on it. Dangling from the machine there is a plastic cup that looks like an anesthesia mask. He places the mask over your genitals. It's freezing, and there's some kind of sticky jelly around the edges. He flips a switch and the machine on the stand starts making noise. It sounds like a muffled recording of whales singing.

"Hear that?" he asks.

Static, white noise.

"Hear what?"

"That bump."

You listen, but you can't tell what you're listening to or what you're listening for.

"What am I listening for?"

"Hold on," the Urologist says, somewhat impatiently. "There. Hear it?"

"Yes?" you lie.

He takes the mask away from your testicles.

"You have a varicocele," he says, writing something down on your chart. "You can go ahead and get dressed now."

"What does that mean?" you ask. You pull your boxers up, but your genitals are a mess of wet sticky goo from the mask. You pretend it's all normal and put your pants on. It feels like you just went swimming in your clothes.

"Do you know what a varicose vein is?"

"You mean like on your legs?"

"Yes. It's like on your legs, but in this case, you have one in your scrotum. What's happened is that the veins supplying blood to your genitals have widened, and there's too much blood. This is elevating the temperature of your testes, which can inhibit normal sperm production. Think of it as if you were always immersed in a hot tub."

"Do you know what caused it?"

"Could be a number of things," he shrugs. "Could be the result of an injury, or it could've been a slight abnormality that's just gotten worse as you've gotten older. You want to fix it though. Eventually it will lead to testicular atrophy."

"That sounds bad."

"It can be quite painful."

"But you *can* fix it?"

"We can repair the vein," he says, still writing in his chart.

"Will that fix my...will that improve my sperm count?"

"Hard to say," he shrugs. "I can tell you I've seen this a lot. There aren't any formal studies, really, but informally? Post-op, 40% of my patients do show dramatic improvements in count, motility, and morphology."

"So...yes?"

"Once the temperature in the scrotum returns to normal, it creates a healthy environment for sperm production. I'd like to schedule you sometime next month if that's convenient. It's a very simple procedure. What we do is we make a small incision in your groin. An inch, an inch-and-a-half," he says, showing you the size with his thumb and index finger.

He tells you all about the procedure. He seems relatively excited about it. There's a small tube inserted. Outpatient. You'll be home the same day. Able to resume work within 24-48 hours. There will be some swelling.

"What you'll want to do is buy a bag of frozen peas."

"Peas?"

"Peas. Or corn. Either one will do."

Of course there are risks with any surgical procedure. Minimal risks. The particular risks associated with this procedure specifically include but are not limited to reactions to anesthesia, infection, artery damage, excessive bleeding, fluid buildup that requires draining, scrotal nerve damage, impotence, and death.

"So this is good news?" you ask. "This will work?"

"There are no guarantees, but you want to do it anyway. In the meantime, you might want to make a few changes to your diet. Eat things high in Folic Acid. Selenium. Can you tolerate pumpkin seeds?"

"Pumpkin seeds?"

"Raw, don't get them roasted. Pumpkin seeds can encourage normal sperm production."

"Really?"

"But get them raw. From a health food store. Okay?"

"Okay," you smile. A bleak curtain has been suddenly lifted. It's all routine. You can fix it. You can solve this problem and be normal again. It's just a bad pipe, some valve that needs replacing. "This is good news, right?"

"Well I'm not going to lie to you. It's not a great time," he says. "You're not going to be able to drive home after the procedure. Do you have someone who can drive you home?"

The sunlight outside the Urologist's office is blinding. You're standing in the parking lot, euphoric on your cellphone, your boxers full of sticky goo, explaining everything to Liesl.

"...so I mean, long story short, he said he can fix it."

"Are you sure?" Liesl asks. "Maybe we should talk to Dr. Greenspan..."

"Dr. Greenspan just wants us to spend twenty-grand on IVF," you say. "If we can fix it, if we can fix it naturally, shouldn't we try that?"

"I'm not saying you shouldn't do it. I'm just saying maybe we should get a second opinion."

"This *is* the second opinion. Dr. Greenspan's the guy who said to see a urologist."

"I mean *another* urologist. This isn't the guy he recommended, right? I mean, Dr. Greenspan did say it was probably irreversible..."

"I'm not going to go see Dr. Greenspan's guy so he can tell me what Dr. Greenspan wants him to. This is the guy in my network. And I can't spend my entire life seeing doctors and going to clinics," you say. "I've got other things to do, you know."

"Other things?" she says. "What could possibly be more important than this? We're talking about *having children*, John. We're talking about our family."

"Why do you think I'm here?!"

"I'm not saying you shouldn't do it, I'm just saying, are there...I mean, is it dangerous?"

"It's totally routine. It's fine. I'll be home the same day."

"And he says it will work?"

"Well I mean nothing is guaranteed, but there's a forty percent chance..."

"I just think we should talk to Dr. Greenspan. I think you should see the man he recommended."

"I thought you'd be happy," you say.

"It's not...I *am* happy, it...I just don't want...I want to be *realistic*, John."

"I'm not being realistic?"

"I just...I know you want to fix this, but maybe you can't...."

"This guy is a *urologist*. He's an expert!"

"But..."

"I gotta do it anyway," you say, angrily. "Otherwise my balls will shrink."

"What?"

"Atrophy. Testicular atrophy."

"Jesus Christ; what is that?"

"That's what happens to people who have this. Your balls

shrivel up."

"Oh," she says.

Silence.

"John, I just don't want you to get your hopes...I'm not trying to...I'm trying to be supportive, I just..."

"Well try a little fucking harder!" you say, and hang up.

THE EVENT PLANNER

For more than twenty-five years, Quill & Pad has employed the Event Planning services of Kathy Apple, or, as she invoices, Kathy Apple, LLC. Recently your accountant has informed you that Kathy Apple is one of the primary beneficiaries of your benefit, a fundraising event that evidently loses the organization $400,000 annually. You have reviewed Ms. Apple's invoices, along with every other invoice, looking for ways to reduce expenses dramatically. If you do not reduce expenses dramatically you will be bankrupt. Ms. Apple is Quill & Pad's most expensive vendor. To manage the Quill & Pad benefit dinner, Ms. Apple charges $500,000 annually. You are taken aback by the roundness of that sum.

This fee does not include the space rental or catering for the event. That is another $250,000 and change. Ms. Apple does not book the speaker, pay for the travel and lodging, print invitations, mail anything, or manage incoming donations. Liquor and decorating are all billed separately.

So you are not quite sure what services Ms. Apple provides for $500,000 a year. Maybe you should be an event planner. It appears to be a great living.

You have never spoken to Ms. Apple directly, as she does not take phone calls. She does not have an email address. Her assistant explains that Ms. Apple does not drive and she will not travel to your office. You must come to her. Ms. Apple does not work downtown, but out of her home in Fairfax County.

You pull up the long gravel driveway to her home, and you wonder if you have the correct address. It appears to be a haunted house. Gangly, spiky green weeds have overtaken the dilapidated front porch, which is badly in need of a paint job. There's a rusted-out Mercedes-Benz parked in front of a garage. The garage door is open. Inside the garage is packed solid with furniture, lamps, bicycles, and all manner of attic crap. There are two metal trashcans on the side of the house, both of which are overflowing with trash. As you walk up the steps you notice that the windows of the house are covered in some kind of sooty film, and when you open the front door, an overwhelming stench of cigarette smoke nearly knocks you over. Inside the foyer there is a small desk, behind which sits a frightened looking twenty-something girl, dressed in a crisp business suit.

"Hi," you say. "I'm sorry, I don't know if I have the right— I'm looking for Kathy Apple?"

"This is the place," the girl says, standing up. "Are you John?"

"Yes."

"I'm Marcy," she says, extending her hand. You shake Marcy's hand as two large golden retrievers bound in from the adjoining dining room. Each of them weighs 100 pounds, and both of them are desperate for your attention. They jump up on you, their tongues hanging out of their mouths, slobbering and shedding all over your suit. Marcy says nothing.

"Uh, hi guys," you say, petting them. This only encourages them. They start barking and shoving their noses in your no-account groin. *Your precious shrinking balls!* The dogs push you back towards the door, their tails wagging.

"Kathy…Miss Apple will be right with you if you just want to…uh…if you just want to wait…" Marcy says. The dogs bark. One of them snakes around behind you.

"Sure," you say, trying to placate the dogs, or at least stop them from attacking you. There's no place to sit down. Even if you could sit you're surrounded by dogs, who continue to bark.

"Did you, uh, can I get you something to drink?" Marcy asks.

"Uh, just a water?" you ask. "Okay, what's *your* name, what's *your* name?" you ask the dogs. The dogs don't answer, and Marcy doesn't help you out. She leaves you in the foyer with the dogs. They're still barking. One of them has his paws on your lapel and the other has his nose in your ass. You're trapped between them. The one in front of you pees on the floor. You stare down at the huge puddle forming on the warped hardwood floor, which creeps towards your dress shoes.

"Okay. Okay. Down, boys, down," you say, but they don't listen. Marcy returns with a Mason Jar full of water.

"Gabriel, Marcus," she says, clapping her hands, and the dogs get down off you. "Sorry about that," she says, handing you the Mason Jar. She grabs the dogs by their collars and leads them into the dining room. She closes two sliding doors, locking them inside. Then she grabs a dishrag from her desk, kneels down in front of you, and begins wiping the pee up. You have the sense that the dishrag is kept for frequent accidents.

You don't know what to do. You don't want to look down at this twenty-year-old girl kneeling in front of you wiping up piss, so you look at your suit instead. You're covered with yellow hair. You take a sip of water from the Mason Jar. It tastes rusty, like the well water you used to drink on the soccer field as a kid.

You're probably not going to drink more of it, but you should, because en route to Kathy Apple's you've eaten about a pound of raw pumpkin seeds to increase your sperm count. You're learning new and exciting lessons about fiber. Your stomach is killing you.

"Sorry. They just get so excited sometimes," Marcy says nervously, depositing the dishrag in a desk drawer and pumping hand sanitizer into her palms. She rubs her hands together nervously. The huge container of hand-sanitizer is half-empty.

You smile at her as she sits back down nervously.

"Are you new?" you ask.

"Me? Oh, yes. I just graduated."

"Congratulations. Where'd you go to school?"

"Cornell," she says.

That sinks in for a minute, as you adjust your laptop bag on your shoulder.

"Ms. Apple will be right down."

*

Ms. Apple meets with you in her weird parlor. There are two couches and smoke-yellowed drapes blocking out the sun. The room is lit by a single Tiffany desk lamp on a credenza. Other than that, the room is littered with bric-a-brac. There's a broken coat rack, an old tricycle with pots of dead plants on the back, several dust-covered banker's boxes, a wooden carving of an elephant that stands six-feet tall. The dogs are allowed into your meeting. You're sinking into one of the plastic covered couches and the dogs are crowding you at the knees, their tails wagging, desperate to sniff your crotch. You keep pushing them away from you. Kathy Apple smokes.

Kathy Apple looks like she might be 170 years old. She carries an ashtray into the meeting, which is already filled to the rim with ash and butts. She is a thin, well-dressed woman who wears several pounds of turquoise jewelry. She reminds you of your childhood piano teacher, who used to rap you on the knuckles with a ruler. Her grey hair is pulled back in a bun so tight it looks like her wrinkled face might snap and roll up at the chin.

"Alice tells me she wants somebody named Hector Siffuentes," she says in a raspy voice.

"Yes," you say.

"I don't know him," she says, tapping her ash, exhaling.

"He's huge in the Gay Latino Poetry community."

"He's a queer?"

"Uh..."

"Marcy!" she screams. Marcy runs in the room. "Where's that book?"

"Which book, Miss Apple?"

"The queer poetry book."

"You just—I just ordered it this morning," Marcy stammers, confused.

"I want it in my hands first thing tomorrow morning."

"Yes ma'am," Marcy says nervously, and exits.

"She's right out of school," Kathy Apple says, rolling her eyes. "You can't do anything with them. You think we can get this Siffuentes guy?"

"I don't see why not."

"Good. Good. The important thing is to keep Alice happy. Alice is happy, we're happy. That's the goal."

"Yes. Well. We have to run the name by the board benefit committee..."

She waves her hand.

"Alice has the only opinion that matters. Get going on booking Siffuentes."

You nod. You are not used to taking orders from a vendor.

"Miss Apple."

"Kathy, honey, call me Kathy," she says, lighting another cigarette. "Where do you hail from?"

"Excuse me?"

"Your background," she says, making a circle with her hand holding the cigarette. "How'd you get here?"

"Well. I worked for the Empire Theater. In Chicago."

"Never heard of it."

"We built a $50 million building on Michigan Avenue," you say, somewhat defensively. "I've got about 15 years of nonprofit management experience...."

"So you're from Chicago."

"Yes."

"Washington ain't Chicago, honey. Let me tell you how this town works," she says, tapping her ash. She points her cigarette at you while she talks. "In this town, the only thing people care about is power. Who's close to power. That's what this benefit is all about. That's how it all works. We give people access to power. It doesn't matter who the speaker is. The only thing that matters is who the table hosts are. Now you got one with Alice, but the rest of your board? They're for shit. They're worthless. They're just a bunch of writers. Well. Except for Algernon, but he's not what he used to be."

"Miss Apple..."

"...and Alice will get you Senator Young, so now you have two. Have you given any thought to the Supreme Court? Don't they have a Mexican now?"

"Uh," you say, somewhat stunned. "I'm sure we'll fill out the table hosts." The dogs are still sniffing at your crotch. "Is there any way we can do this without the dogs?"

"You don't like dogs?" she asks, somewhat surprised. Then she claps her hand. "Gabriel. Marcus. Outside."

The dogs listen to her, and they scamper off to some other corner of the house.

"Not a dog lover?" she asks.

"Miss Apple...Kathy, seeing as how this will be my first benefit, I'd like to run down the schedule with you."

"The schedule? It's not rocket science. Reception, dinner, speaker, dessert..."

"No, not the evening itself, I mean leading up to it. I'd like to talk about the schedule leading up...I just want to go over some logistics."

"I don't do schedules."

"Well, maybe for my sake, we could..."

"I've done this thirty years without a schedule."

"Well, just so I can understand..."

"We don't need a schedule."

That seems to be the end of the discussion.

"Okay," you say. "Well then, I'd like to run down the budget with you."

"Budget's your end. That's your deal. I don't do budgets."

"Yes, well, Kathy, I'm trying to figure out...this is going to be a difficult year for us, and we need to...we need to maximize our revenue..."

"As opposed to every other year?"

"Kathy—"

She waves you off.

"Look, it's pretty simple, Jack. There are fifty-five ten-tops, 550 seats, a thousand bucks each, the key is selling a few tables and getting a couple big sponsors at the $25,000 and $50,000 level. You want to walk away with about a million. A million bucks is a lot of money."

"Yes. Well. About that, see, I've run down the expenses, and we're actually spending more than a million just to throw the benefit."

"No," she says, shaking her head. "You're wrong."

"Well, actually...it's all right here. And that doesn't even include my salary, or the staff's. I've broken it down here, if you just..."

She shakes her head.

"I know the expenses every year, and I know you clear at least a hundred grand."

"Well, yes. Before your expenses are added in, that's right. Afterwards we're short about four hundred thousand."

"Well I have to be paid. I provide a service here."

"Um, and can you tell me what that is?"

"What what is?"

"Can you tell me...do we have a letter of agreement that lists the services you provide in exchange for the fee?"

"Oh honey, you don't understand how this town works," she says.

You are tired of people explaining cities to you.

"Yeah, well, I understand that most fundraisers actually generate revenue for the organization," you say. "So, you know, generally speaking, when I've organized fundraisers in the past, I like to generate more revenue than expenses. I like to raise funds. Hence the term. Fundraiser."

You manage a smile for Kathy, who lights another cigarette.

"You're looking at this thing all wrong. You should call Vanessa and talk to her, and she can explain it to you..."

"Kathy, I think we really need to be on the same page about this—I'm here to tell you, we really don't have the money to do this anymore. I'm not going to raise money so I can pay for a party."

"Excuse me?"

"Our other grants, for the charitable work we do, for the education program, for the kids, for literature—some of that

66

money's been going to fund this benefit. To pay your fee. And if we're going to do that, I need to have a good handle on what services we can expect for that fee."

"I need to bring Alice in on this conversation."

Then she gets up and walks out. You sit there for a few minutes, not knowing if the meeting is over.

It is over.

BUBBLES

You lay in the bathtub thinking about bankruptcy and infertility. You stare at your balls. They look all right. They seem to work normally. You've never had a problem getting an erection. If you tried hard enough, you could get one right now. Hell, you could shoot a load all over the place. You could paint the walls. Generally you find that a pleasant and rewarding experience. But you don't feel like it at the moment.

It just doesn't seem right. All the mechanisms and signals seem to function normally. Yet there is nothing there, nothing but dead sperm and not a lot of it. Suddenly you're fourteen again, buying your first condoms at the drug store, throwing a toothbrush and a copy of *Time* magazine in there to make it seem casual, getting dirty looks from the old lady behind the counter. Looks like you didn't need that experience! Looks like the collected sum of twenty dollars you've expended on rubbers was a wasted investment. What if you'd invested that money in the stock market?

Maybe God is punishing you. Maybe he hates your weakness, your cowardice, and your fear. Maybe it's for being a smug little prick in high school, or a morose lonely pot-smoker in college. Maybe it was the pot. It had to be the pot. Maybe it was all that jerking off, all those twisted fantasies and your staunch commitment to a life of sin. And you hope God does hate you, because if he doesn't, the world is a much more terrifying place.

If nothing is done there will be an end to you, to everything you are. You will live a barren existence, and commit your wife to a barren existence. Perhaps you will succeed financially. Perhaps not. You will acquire property, see the latest movies, see the world. You will awaken at noon on Sundays with nowhere to go and nothing to do.

Something tells you that's not going to work. She'll put up with a lot. She'll put up with your crazy job and your stubbornness, but you can't ask her to give up children. God or no God, there's something in the universe that wants more of her. And you're standing in the way.

You've crapped eight times today from eating too many raw pumpkin seeds. The bathroom is filled with your stink but it's yours, so what the hell. Now you're taking a bubble bath. You need a bubble bath. You'd also like another beer.

You are wondering just what you should do at this point in your life's journey. You have not yet informed Liesl of the financial problems at Quill & Pad. You have not informed her that you have cut your own salary by 10%. You have not yet told her that you have dragged her across the country away from her family and her job only to throw her into millions of dollars of potential liability.

Of course you could always quit and take your chances. On the other hand, you are thirty-eight years old, with no professional degree, in the worst economy since the Great Depression. You are the proud owner of a Chicago townhome that is worth $150,000 less than when you purchased it. Your renters barely cover the mortgage payment, and they've been complaining about the furnace. You also have two car payments and sizable student loan debt. No one in their right mind would hire an Executive Director or a Development Director who was let go from his previous job, and then quit two months after taking another job. Your career would be over.

Of course your career is likely over no matter what you do. It doesn't matter who lied. It doesn't matter what the financial statements said or didn't say. You imagine an interview process something like this:

"So, can you tell me why you left your previous position after only two months?"

"I discovered rampant financial fraud."

"You're hired."

But it really wouldn't matter if you quit. You don't need a lawyer to tell you that. The impending financial tsunami at Quill & Pad is nothing compared to the ignominy that will be heaped upon you. If you leave it will all unravel very quickly; the story will come out. It's not going to make the evening news but the right people will know what happened at Quill & Pad. You'll never work in the arts again, that's for sure. You'll be finished. Your name dragged through the mud, stained with their problems forever. Seventeen years of clawing and scratching and sweat down the drain. You know how hard it is to make a decent living in this business.

And even if you quit it won't matter in the end. You'll still get the blame when the whole thing goes tits up. When the lawsuits come. Nonprofit organizations are generally required to maintain Directors and Officers policies, which would provide legal help to you in the event of lawsuits. That legal help would not be provided in the case of fraud. Fraud isn't your only problem. At the end of the year the company will owe real people real money. Landlords. Utilities. Banks. Then there's the IRS. People will want to be paid.

They will sue everyone and anyone.

The staff, Jesus, the staff. A bunch of twenty-somethings who depend on you. What are you going to tell them? What are you going to tell the Education Coordinator who moved from Iowa and lives in a shitty studio apartment in DuPont? There's no money for your studio, kid. There's no money for your health insurance. Here's two weeks pay, now get out.

On paper, you know there is only one way out, one way to save your career and move on. You need to stick it out for a year, raise a million dollars, look like a superstar, and jump ship as fast as you possibly can.

You have no idea how to do that. If you don't do it, you're riding the barrel all the way over the waterfall.

You wonder how you should broach this topic with Liesl. *Hey, I know it's my fault we can't have a family, and by the way, in twelve months we're going to be disgraced and bankrupt. Can we move in with your parents?*

Liesl is supposed to be grading essays but she isn't. You can hear her crying in the bedroom. The door is shut. She's pretending that you can't hear. You're pretending that you don't.

#47

In the morning you visit Algernon Albert, the Board Treasurer, a billionaire businessman who's been on the board for twenty-eight years. You're not entirely sure what Algernon Albert does, but he docs own his own office building on K Street. He is one of the wealthiest men in Washington, DC His Washingtonian Power-Broker Profile (#47) merely describes him as a financial genius.

Despite this reputation, Algernon Albert has allowed Quill & Pad to operate in a huge deficit for several years without noticing, and, in his official capacity as Corporate Secretary, he has affixed his signature and legal guarantee to several fraudulent statements to the Internal Revenue Service. Mr. Albert manages Quill & Pad's endowment, which has now dwindled down to a mere $40,000. The account is so small it's barely worth talking about. Despite having rich experiences in life, you have never declared bankruptcy, so you are not entirely sure how it works. But you have put together a timeline you find useful and somewhat reasonable.

The first thing that will happen is that all the staff, including you, will be quickly terminated, or, if nobody bothers to terminate you, then at the very least you will stop getting paid. Your health insurance benefits will also cease.

Within thirty days your landlord will wonder what's happened to the $45,000 monthly payment you make on your auditorium and offices. You have been an excellent tenant for decades. Certainly they will understand for a few days. Then one day they will stop understanding. Locks will be changed, evictions will be issued, and you will no longer have access to the building. You are unsure of what happens to the actual physical assets in Quill & Pad's possession. Probably best to get the computers and files out prior to the shitstorm.

Soon after this, rumors will begin to circulate about financial troubles at the venerable Quill & Pad, taken over just months ago by a young kid from Chicago nobody's ever heard of. The word "improprieties" will be used. These will be only rumors at first, until a small piece appears in the *Post*, which will be followed soon after by a bigger piece. "What happened at Quill & Pad?" Furious employees and everyone with a grudge against you or Quill & Pad will scream off the record about horrible goings-on at the old sawhorse.

Then it will hit *The Atlantic* or *The New Yorker*, and then you're really doomed, because the board will begin running for cover. Blame will be assigned, primarily to you, by people whose megaphones and bank accounts are much, much larger than yours.

At this point the IRS will get involved, and the Inspectors General at the National Endowment for the Arts and the National Endowment for the Humanities will send fairly innocuous letters using the word "inquiry." Everyone will have some reasonable questions you cannot answer. But you can't receive these notices because you're not in your office anymore. There will be some question about whether or not the organization must return its federal grants, totaling more than $125,000 in the previous year alone.

Around the same time, people will begin to sue the organization, and, as one of the Corporate Officers, with signatory powers over most of the organization's accounts, you will be named personally. You will now need to retain a lawyer.

Now you will be on your own, without an income, sued by millionaires and pursued by several different agencies of the Federal government, with the press lined up against you and all the board running for the hills. Then some famous, beloved American author will pen an opinion piece for the *New York Times* about this saddest of days in American Letters.

And today, in your first meeting with Algernon Albert, allegedly the 47th most powerful man in Washington, you get to share all this good news, and then ask for an enormous amount of money. You park your Golf beneath the building, in the cramped and packed parking lots so familiar to you now. You check to see if there's anything in your teeth. You dust off the pumpkin seeds from your binder on the passenger seat, the one with all your charts and memos explaining what happened, with all your probing and accusatory questions, and you make your way to the lobby.

A large cathedral would fit inside the lobby of Albert Enterprises. There is nothing at all in the lobby except marble floors, marble benches, and a tiny, circular reception desk, at which sits a man in a security uniform. He is watching a set of black and white monitors concealed by the desk.

"Sign in, please," he says, without looking at you. You sign your name to a clipboard, and he directs you to an elevator that will take you to the tenth floor. The tenth floor is the top floor. By Federal Law, nothing in the whole city can be taller than the Washington Monument. This farsighted policy is primarily the reason why rents are astronomical in Washington, DC, and why it suffers from crippling traffic. No one who works in DC can actually afford to live in DC, including you. You drive an hour each way.

Algernon Albert's tenth floor suite is quite spacious and inviting. It's clean and modern looking, all double-height glass windows and white walls, with two tasteful couches in front of the receptionist's desk. The receptionist's name is Cindy. She is an Administrative Assistant, not a receptionist. Tea, coffee, water? Nothing for you, thanks.

There is a massive piece of modern art hanging on the wall behind Cindy, a mess of colored, squiggly lines. You don't like modern art. You're not sure what it's supposed to be or why anyone would bother with it. You prefer paintings where you understand what you are looking at. But as you sit on the couch you begin to appreciate this mess of colors, the way it adds so much to the sterile lobby of Albert Enterprises.

An ancient, rumpled-looking man appears from around the corner and leans down behind Cindy. He looks shriveled and he walks slowly, as if he has something metal in both of his legs. He is a clean-shaven man with thin grey hair, withered and wrinkled, with giant brillo pads of surprisingly black hair erupting from his ears. Cindy nods to you and whispers in his ear, and then he nods and shuffles slowly over to you. You stand up.

"Are you Jack?" he asks, offering you his hand.

"John, sir."

"John. Come on back. Come on back,"

You follow Algernon Albert back behind Cindy's desk, and you have to walk very, very slowly so you don't run into him. It takes about six minutes to travel the twenty feet to Albert's office. There are family pictures on the wall, including a gigantic oil-portrait of a beautiful young woman.

"Have a seat," he says. "You're here to see me...?"

"Uh, for Quill & Pad, sir."

"Yes, yes. Quill & Pad. Yes. That's right," he says, carefully easing into his chair. There is a computer behind him. "You're Hillary's replacement?"

"I'm sorry?"

"Hillary?"

"Uh. You mean Vanessa, the previous Executive?"

"Yes, yes. Vanessa. That's right. Vanessa. How is Alice?"

"Alice? Uh, I think she's fine, sir."

"Well, send her my best," he says. "Her father and I go way back, you know. Fought in the Battle of Saipain."

"Yes, sir."

He taps his fingers on his desk, nods and smiles at you.

"Did you find the building all right?"

"Oh, yes. Yes, sir. Hard to miss, really."

"It can be terrible getting around this city. I hope you didn't drive."

"It's not so bad."

"Did you drive?"

"Uh, yes. Yes. I did."

"We have parking, you know," he says. "Cindy can validate your parking."

"Thank you, sir."

"Yes," he says. "It's almost intolerable anymore. Don't you think it's intolerable?"

"Yes, sir," you smile.

"Yes," he says. "Are you married, Jack?"

"Yes, yes I am."

"Kids?"

"No, not yet sir."

"No?" he asks. "I have five of them. You should have kids. Get cracking! There's never a good time. How is Alice?"

"Um. She's fine, sir. I saw her a few weeks ago. Well. She

seemed fine."

"Good. Yes," he says. "Her father and I go way back. Fought in the Battle of Saipain. Oh. Wait. Have you seen this?"

He turns around to face his computer monitor, and he hunts and pecks on the keyboard. He seems to be frustrated, and then he calls out, "Cindy," feebly.

"Cindy?" he asks. "Cindy?"

You're certain that Cindy can't hear him.

"Would you like me to get Cindy?" you ask.

"Yes, would you run and fetch her? I want her to show me that video I was watching."

You get up and get Cindy.

"What's he asking for?" she asks.

"He says there's a video he was watching?"

"Oh good lord," she says, rolling her eyes.

Cindy walks back with you to Albert's office, where he is hunting and pecking at the keyboard.

"Is everything all right, Mr. Albert?" she asks rather loudly.

"I can't get that video to show up. I want to show Jack here that video I was watching."

"It's John, sir," she says, a little louder. "Now what can I help you find, Mr. Albert?"

"The video, the video! The one Gary sent me this morning."

"Did he send you an email?" Cindy asks, leaning over him, taking over the keyboard.

"Yes, I got it from the e-mail," he says. "I want to show Jack the video Gary sent me."

"John, sir," Cindy says, opening his email. "From Quill & Pad."

She scrolls down a few pages of messages until she apparently finds Gary's email. The email is not from this month, let alone this morning. The video opens up.

"Is that the one?"

"No, no, the other one was bigger."

"We can make it bigger, Mr. Albert," she assures him. "You just click here."

"Well make it bigger. Turn the sound up," he says, waving his arms in an upward swing, to motion *bigger, louder*. Cindy obliges, and steps back from the computer so you can see. "Wait until you see this," he says. "You'll get a kick out of this, Jack!"

It's an Arabic website. There's Arabic writing above the video. The camera is shaky and you can hear a crowd screaming. There's smoke, dust, and suddenly you see two Middle-Eastern men dragging a man in a brown military uniform through the dust. The military man's pants are around his ankles, and his face is bruised and bloody. It takes you a moment to realize that the man is dead. There is a small hole about the size of a nickel on his temple. The other men keep shouting in Arabic, and then a teenage kid shows up with a lead pipe. The kid inserts the pipe into the dead man's rectum as the crowd cheers.

This goes on for an ungodly amount of time.

"They got the son of a bitch," Mr. Albert says, making a celebratory fist. "What do you think of that, Jack? They got the son of a bitch. They finally got him."

You don't know what to say to that, and you look at Cindy, who looks upwards and gives a very subtle shrug.

"Mr. Albert, this is John MacManus. He's here from Quill & Pad."

"Quill & Pad, right. Yes. Good," he says, rapping his fingers on the desk again. "Are you Hillary's replacement?"

"Can you validate my parking?" you whisper to Cindy.

GHOSTS

You have the Accountant on the phone. The Accountant does not like your phone calls, but he can't avoid them now, either. You know this and he knows this. You're in this together. If Quill & Pad goes down, there are going to be embarrassing questions about a very high-profile accounting firm, and especially about the lead accountant on the job, and that's not the most direct path to making partner. You are asking him how to wrestle away control of your remaining investments from the 47th most powerful man in Washington, who seems to be suffering from Alzheimer's disease.

"I don't see what you can do," the Accountant sighs. "He's the sole signatory on the account."

"Can we get him declared incompetent?"

"Sure. If you want to sue him. Good luck with that."

Your other line blinks.

"I'll call you back," you say.

"Oh goody," the Accountant says. You flip over to the other line.

"Hold the line for Mrs. Cavanaugh-Williams," a voice says.

You can't tell if it's a man or a woman. There are a few beeps and cracks, and then you are connected with Alice Cavanaugh-Williams, who appears to be calling from Times Square. You hear cars, wind, and horns.

"John?" she yells.

"Mrs. Cavanaugh-Williams?" you ask.

"What did you say to Kathy Apple?" she asks curtly. "Taxi!"

"I had a meeting with her and..."

"Who told you to have a meeting with Kathy Apple?"

"Uh..."

"You don't meet with Kathy Apple. I meet with Kathy Apple. Taxi!"

"Yes, I needed to..."

"The Hilton please, thank you," she says, and you hear a cab door shut. "John, I'm trying very hard to understand what happened. Can you tell me what happened?"

"Yes, I met with Kathy to discuss the benefit."

"She said you called her a liar?"

"What?"

"She's *incensed*. She's threatening to pull out of the event."

"I assure you I didn't call her a liar."

"John, I don't think you understand how this town works," she says. "I'm very disappointed that I have to deal with this."

"All I said was..."

"I'm going to make this as clear as I possibly can for you," she says. "I want you to understand me. You are not to call Kathy Apple without my express permission. Do you understand me?"

"I can't call the event planner?"

"She's not an event planner, John. She's a friend of this organization, and she's been a friend since before you were born. You are out of your depth here. I asked you if you understood what I was telling you. Do you understand what I'm telling you?"

"You don't want me to speak with Kathy Apple."

"Yes. For anything. Under any circumstances. Are we clear? I deal with Kathy."

"I understand."

"You are not to contact her."

"I got it."

"Good. I'm sorry we had to have a conversation like this. I don't want to have conversations like this."

"Me neither," you say. "I'm sorry if I offended you, or…"

"Where are we with Hector Siffuentes?"

"I have a call with his assistant in an hour," you say. "We'll get him."

"Concentrate on that. Let me know when it's done. We're clear on Kathy Apple."

"Very clear," you say. "But Mrs. Cavanaugh-Williams, I think we need to talk about the finances…"

"That's Algernon's business. I don't get involved in those conversations."

"Well, it's…there are serious problems to…"

"Call Algernon."

"Yes, I met with Algernon this morning, and…"

"You met with Algernon?"

"Yes. I had to talk to him because…"

"Who told you to meet with Algernon?"

"Uh…but…I thought…"

"I think we need to have some clarity on your role here at Quill & Pad," she says. "I want you to set up a meeting of the Executive Committee next week. Tuesday morning is good. We can do it at my house."

And then she hangs up.

You slam the phone down. Well this is just great. Fuck Mrs. Alice Cavanaugh-Williams and her radishes and her bitch meeting planner. Fuck Quill & Pad and their goddamned…

Wait a minute.

Are they going to *fire* you? Are they seriously going to fire you? You've been here two months. You moved across the damn country into a burning trainwreck. Suddenly there's a pit in your stomach. Fired? What happens to you when you're fired? You feel sick. What are you going to tell Liesl? What are you going to do? In this economy?

Then suddenly:

Wait.

What if they *do* fire you?

What if they fire you two months into your tenure?

Maybe that could actually be the best possible way out of this mess. You have a two-year contract. If you resign, that's different, but if you're fired? They'd have to pay you out the remainder, and right now, they can do that. *You* can do that. In a perverse bit of good luck, you'd be legally *obliged* to do that, and you'd have access to the accounts to make the disbursement. And not just your salary, but your health care, your vacation, your retirement contributions, all of it. Quick, back-of-the envelope math gets you a lump sum just shy of $250,000 before taxes. That'd take the sting out, wouldn't it? They could sue you, but you'd absolutely be covered under the Directors & Officers policy in that instance, and in the end, you'd win. And these people aren't going to blink at that kind of money. They kennel their dogs for that kind of scratch.

But even better than the money, if they're going to fire you—and you *know* they're going to fire you—then you can control the narrative. You'd have a few months where you'd be radioactive, where nobody on earth would hire you—but then? Once the wheels come off the car, you could paint yourself as the truth-teller who warned of impending doom only to be cut down for daring to speak.

You know the right people in this world to whisper to. And the best part is, they don't even seem to know the hole they're in.

Time to explain it to them. And now you even have the perfect forum: the Executive Committee meeting. Who the hell is on the Executive Committee? That sounds official. You can send each member of the Executive Committee a huge, scathing memo describing the malfeasance that has occurred and the doom that is looming over Quill & Pad. A nice, long, written report, distributed from your personal email account to each officer of the board, detailing every single problem you've uncovered in your two months at Quill & Pad. Something you can conveniently leak once the ship goes down.

Your phone rings. You're so caught up with your brilliant evil scheme to orchestrate your own termination that you've almost forgotten about your call with Hector Siffuentes's personal assistant. The most important thing now is to be absolutely on the ball. Answer every call, show up fifteen minutes early, stay two hours late each day, make sure you do everything according to Hoyle...you have to be unimpeachable, perfect.

"John MacManus," you say.

"Mr. MacManus, this is Nadia Kinder. I'm calling on behalf of Mr. Siffuentes?"

"Nadia, thanks for calling back," you smile. "Did you have a chance to review our offer letter?"

"Yes, uh, it is very generous," Nadia says, as if reading from a script. She sounds young and nervous.

"Well, we're all very excited to welcome Mr. Siffuentes to the Quill & Pad Benefit."

"Thank you," Nadia says, and you hear some shuffling papers. "Mr. Siffuentes is happy to appear at your event, but I wanted to make you aware of some special arrangements that need to be made before we finalize the contract."

You lean back in your chair. You've dealt with difficult artists before.

"Sure," you say. "What can we do to make Mr. Siffuentes comfortable?"

You hear a man speaking lowly to Nadia on the other end of the phone. Then Nadia whispers something back. Then she returns.

"Mr. Siffuentes requires three, twenty-ounce bottles of Poland Spring sparkling water to be available at the podium," Nadia says.

"Not a problem," you say, scribbling down the request on a scratch pad.

"Lime flavor, please," she says.

"Lime it is."

"It's very important. He's allergic to most lemon flavoring. It gives him hives."

"I will have lime water standing by."

"He would prefer one single light on stage, from the top, and behind. Please no direct spotlight on Mr. Siffuentes, as he has very sensitive skin."

"Can do."

"Book signings can sometimes be a problem for Mr. Siffuentes. He needs to be assured that reasonable precautions will be taken to ensure his security."

"I can assure you, we'll have a crack team of commandos standing by," you joke. The crowd will be filled with grey-haired millionaires. You're not that concerned for Mr. Siffuentes's safety. As big as he may be in the Gay Latino Poetry Community.

"In his introduction, please advise the audience that Mr. Siffuentes does not accept gifts from those who want their books signed."

"Well…"

"Mr. Siffuentes will sign books for forty-five minutes following the reading. It's best if those waiting to have their books signed are given post-it notes beforehand, so they can clearly print the inscription they would like in their books. This will ensure that as many people as possible get their books signed."

"Uh, I will definitely see what I can do on that front, but typically we don't do signings following the benefit."

There is a pause.

"There won't be book sales?"

"Well, this is a black tie event, a seated dinner," you explain. "There's really not an opportunity for that kind of thing. We buy copies of the book for each guest beforehand. They're party favors. We'll introduce him, then he reads for about twenty minutes, then we seat him for dinner. That's it."

You hear Nadia, her voice muffled, explaining what you've said to somebody in the room.

"Okay," she says. "Mr. Siffuentes will also require somebody to be on hand to escort him out from the event, so he does not appear rude when he leaves."

"I'll be there for the duration, and I can take him back to his room when the time is up. Don't worry. I'm good at being the bad guy."

"Thank you. Mr. Siffuentes also requires an adjoining hotel room for his ghost."

Over the years, you have managed several strange requests. But this is new.

"Excuse me?"

"Mr. Siffuentes is haunted by the ghost of his future self," Nadia explains. "His ghost requires adjoining accommodation at the hotel."

You're not quite sure what to say, and you're stifling the

urge to laugh. "You know, we've secured a very nice suite for Mr. Siffuentes at the Ritz Carlton. It's very spacious. I've toured the hotel myself, and there are two bedrooms in the suite. It's very nice. They have amazing cookies."

"I'm afraid that is insufficient," Nadia says. "As I said, he will also require the adjoining hotel room for his ghost."

"Well, I, uh...I'll certainly see what I can do about that—I'm not sure there is an adjoining room available. I'm a bit at the mercy of the hotel..."

"I'm afraid he really must insist."

"Well," you sigh. You have never reserved a room for a ghost. "I'm sure we can figure that out."

"Please have keys for this room brought up to Mr. Siffuentes's room prior to the reading," Nadia says.

"Absolutely," you say, scribbling the note down. A suite at the Ritz Carlton in DC costs $3,200 a night, and you're fairly certain that securing additional lodging will cost another $3,200. On top of Mr. Siffuentes's preposterous $20,000 honoraria and his first-class plane ticket, this speaker is going to run nearly $40,000, which is exactly $40,000 more than you have to spend.

"Nadia, just so I'm clear," you say. "This ghost is an older version of Mr. Siffuentes?"

"That is correct."

You are too amazed to respond with anything clever. Eventually, several troubling logistical questions will occur to you. Where does the ghost live when Mr. Siffuentes is at home? How does the ghost travel to Mr. Siffuentes's various speaking engagements? Through the spectral realm? If the ghost is Mr. Siffuentes's future self, then isn't he really a time traveler? Shouldn't he have access to important information about the future?

"Are we agreed?" Nadia asks.

PART THREE

SHARED PROMISE

The fertility clinic is not like other doctors' offices. The waiting room is beautiful and spacious, but it's not crowded. A woman asks you if you'd like anything to drink. No need to fill out the insurance forms—this is just a friendly consultation.

The fifty-two inch flatscreen TV hanging in the corner plays a video on a loop. *The Conception Journey.* The actress delivering the voiceover is vaguely familiar, but you can't place her. She's famous, though, in that second-tier of fame—the people you recognize in bit parts on cop shows and sitcoms.

"Every journey is different, and each poses challenges, but whatever the path, Shared Promise can help you reach your destination. Our cutting edge technology and world-class physicians have helped thousands of families achieve their dreams."

Bill and Jess appear on the screen. They're a normal-looking couple. Bill's wearing a blue sweater and khakis. Jess is wearing a dress. They're sitting in a nice suburban living room on a leather couch, and nestled between them is their adorable baby girl, Adelia.

"We'd lost hope," Jess says, playing with Adelia's hands.

"When we came to Shared Promise, we really thought we were out of options."

"Shared Promise worked out a payment plan that worked for our family," Bill interjects weirdly.

"Mr. and Mrs. MacManus?" a nurse asks, smiling. She has giant white teeth. She's not a nurse. She's a Fertility Consultant. She looks fantastic. She wears an immaculate white labcoat over a pressed blue dress. Not a blond hair out of place. She looks like she was molded somewhere. She looks like she gets fourteen hours of sleep a night. "I'm Shirley. Why don't you come on back?"

You follow Shirley back to the Consultation Room. There is no desk in the consultation room. There are two couches and a coffee table, a marble-topped credenza and a black refrigerator. There are three bottles of Evian on the coffee table.

"Dr. Greenspan will join us in just a few moments, but first I just wanted to talk to you about how you're doing."

Your wife tells Shirley how you're doing. As she speaks Shirley crosses her legs and leans in, nodding, looking sympathetic. Liesl catalogs all the tests and procedures and indignities over the previous twelve months. She starts to cry. Shirley talks about support group services that are available.

"I'm sorry," Liesl says. It's then that you notice that there's a box of tissues on the coffee table. They've thought of everything at Shared Promise. "I'm sorry."

"No, no, no," Shirley says, putting her hand on your wife's knee, calling her by her name. "Liesl, one thing people don't understand about this journey is the *psychological* toll it takes on everyone involved. You should be upset. Because it's upsetting. It's perfectly normal to be upset."

"It's just, that...god, look at me," Liesl says, trying to pull it together. "Last week my sister called me, and she's pregnant, again—it's her second, and I want to be happy for her, I do, but—

all I feel is…I just feel so *angry*. Not at John, I mean, it's not his fault…"

But it is your fault. If it's not your fault, whose fault is it? Why couldn't it be her fault? But that's an ugly thought. You keep having ugly thoughts. You keep trying to be rational, to understand. Of course she's angry with you. You're angry with you.

"It's just so *unfair*."

"It is unfair," Shirley says. "One of the things we hear a lot from couples in your situation is how powerless they feel. But you know, it's nothing you did. And my understanding is, well the good news is, you guys have a ton of options."

"We do?" Liesl asks.

"Sure. The most important factor in conception is the health and age of the mother, and you're young, you're in great shape, and you have a very, very healthy reproductive system."

At this point Dr. Greenspan enters, carrying a large manila file folder. You stand up; he shakes your hand. He sits down next to Shirley. He looks very doctorly as he spreads out a number of charts and reports on the table.

"So let's see where we're at," he says. "I see you went to visit Dr. Mukherjee; I have his recommendation here. Looks like you've gone ahead and scheduled the varicocele repair, is that right?"

"Yes," you say.

"He said that would help," Liesl offers.

Dr. Greenspan nods, picks up a piece of paper and studies it for a moment, then folds his hands together.

"Well Dr. Mukherjee is a fine urologist," he says. "I think that regardless of the impact on fertility it's probably advisable to go ahead and have the procedure."

"But will it help?" Liesl asks.

He winces. He tries to frame his answer carefully.

"There's not a lot of clinical information on the impact of these procedures on male infertility," he says. "I know that in some cases, it has been shown to improve the count and the motility, but those improvements have not been consistent, and they're generally marginal. I think—as I said, there are other reasons to have the procedure, but if you're asking me if you should put your conception hopes in this basket, my advice would be to seriously start considering some other options for your conception journey."

You wish people would stop using words like "conception journey." You don't like Dr. Greenspan. You think he's trying to snooker you, like some carnival barker selling you snake oil. You think he sees your crying wife and smells money. You like Dr. Mukherjee, with his office full of boner pills, much more than this man, who hands you a brochure on In Vitro Fertilization, which is not covered by your insurance, which costs more than a mid-sized sedan, and which will finally confirm that you're a failure as a man.

"Look, as I said, the good news is, you do have some viable sperm," Dr. Greenspan continues. "My advice, given your age, given where we're at, and what I'm hearing from you both, is to begin the IVF process now. One of the risks associated with varicocele repair—and it's a marginal risk, I'm not trying to scare you—but there's the potential that it could actually make things worse."

"What?" Liesl says.

"It's very rare, I'm not saying you shouldn't do it, there are other reasons to do it, but before you begin that process, I would collect a sample and proceed with an IVF cycle. Then, John, I would go ahead and have the procedure."

"Wait, it could make things *worse*?" Liesl says.

"Probably it's not going to make a difference," Dr. Greenspan says, waving his hands. "But you are going to lose a few months, potentially. Listen, why don't you both go home, review the information on IVF, talk about it, and let's revisit this in a couple days."

Dr. Greenspan's brochure has been designed by the very best. No expense has been spared. Fold-outs, pocket folders with custom inserts, high quality stock, a premium varnish, happy smiling couples in staged photos talking about their goddamned conception journeys. Babies.

You know how much a printed piece like this cost: at least eight dollars apiece in a low-quantity, high-quality sheet-fed press. More than a *New York Times* bestseller costs to produce. There might be three presses in the District that can handle a job this sophisticated. It claims to be an informational brochure, but this is a sales piece, even if the numbers aren't laid down. That will be provided after you've made your decision and signed whatever you have to sign. Then you will deal with representatives and middle-aged women in cubicles who never return your phone calls.

But for now you're in the comfort and safety of the Consultation Room, where Shirley is smiling and offering you Evian.

"Of course, this is your decision," she says.

*

In the parking lot of Shared Promise you're arguing with your wife. You're both sitting in the front of your Volkswagen Golf, staring out the windshield at an Embassy Suites.

"I just don't understand what your problem is," she says from the passenger seat. You both have your seatbelts on, as if you are about to leave, but you're not going anywhere. Not for a while. "He didn't say you shouldn't fix it."

"I just think we should see how it goes first and then see

about IVF," you say. "What if it works?"

"And what if it doesn't?" she asks. "What if it makes it worse? What if we can't do anything then? Seriously, John, how long are we going to wait before we have kids? We can't wait forever. I'm not going to wait forever."

"Don't be so dramatic," you snap. Why are you so angry with her? You shouldn't be this angry, but you feel hot and out of control.

"Dramatic?!" she laughs, exasperated. She shakes her head, exhales deeply, tries to keep from screaming at you.

"All I'm saying is, is this really the best time to think about this, Liesl?"

"What?"

"I mean leaving this aside, the timing—do you *know* what I'm going through at work? Do you understand what's happening? Do you know what would happen if I suddenly lost my job? We wouldn't be able to afford *rent*, let alone twenty-five grand for this. Where's that going to come from? Where's it going to come from, Liesl? Because a teacher's salary isn't gonna cut it!"

She takes it all in, and inhales, and then shuts her eyes.

She is better than you. She takes a moment after you finish your lecture before she responds.

"I really think you need to see somebody, John," she says.

"See somebody? When am I going to find time to—"

"This can't go on like this. I can't. When was the right time? Was it last year in Chicago? It was like you were married to your job—"

"I'm trying to get ahead! I'm trying to think about our *future!*"

"*What future?!*" she screams, slams her hand on the glove compartment. "Christ almighty, I am *so sick* of hearing about your *fucking job*. I don't care anymore. You don't think I'm thinking about the future? We're going to have a future where somebody pays you ten thousand dollars more and we move across the country, away from our friends, our family—*I'm* thinking about the future. I'm the *only one* thinking about it. This is the rest of our lives, John. Do you understand that? It's *my* life, too. You can't do this because of your job? Quit your job. Find another job. You hate it! I don't care if you go work in a Starbucks. And what, it's my fault teachers get paid in beans? Talk to a fucking congressman."

"Well *somebody* in this relationship has to think about money!" you scream. "And don't tell me it's going to be twenty-five grand, because it's going to be a lot more than that, I promise you. What if it doesn't even work? What then? Then we're right back here and now we're broke? We're already broke. We'll just be broker."

"Oh my god, you are such a condescending prick!" she says, slamming the dashboard with her hand. "You don't think I know what it costs? That price covers three cycles, John," she says, slapping the brochure. "Three full cycles."

"Great!" you say, throwing your hands up. "Is it buy two, get one free? Look at this fucking brochure! You know how much a brochure like this costs? They don't care about us. They don't care about me, or our problems, or the fact that we can't have a baby. They care about one thing: money. That's all. That's it. And this fucking brochure—I feel like we're buying a car! This is a baby. This is a *baby* we're talking about..."

"OF COURSE IT'S A BABY!" she yells, and then she just shakes her head, puts her head in her hands, and screams into them. "You keep talking about the future. Money. What does money matter? There is no future without this. Do I really have to argue with you about it? I don't care what your problem is at work, I'm sick of hearing about it—I love you, John, but get your head out of your ass."

Then she gets out of the car.

"Liesl," you say, rolling down the window.

"I'm gonna call a cab. You figure out what you wanna do, and you let me know. Asshole."

ANACOSTIA

In six days you will meet with the Executive Committee, which will likely fire you. This will be the best possible outcome you can hope for. It will occur following a procedural motion. The meeting will begin with an update on the Benefit, in which you can assure the board that you've secured the presence of a celebrated but haunted Gay Latino Poet. This will be followed by new business, in which the organization's biggest donor will express her profound dissatisfaction with your performance over the last sixty days. A motion will be made to approve your dismissal from the organization. You will be asked to leave the room, and when you come back in, you will no longer be employed.

And so, before the meeting takes place in the sitting room of Alice Cavanaugh-Williams, you must send the Executive Committee a suicide note known as a Strategic Plan. This document will articulate the wacky hijinks and shenanigans that have apparently occurred at Quill & Pad over the last five years, including fraud, gross financial mismanagement, lying to the IRS, and misusing various charitable gifts and funds.

These practices are generally no-nos in the nonprofit world.

You may also note that the organization's remaining cash assets seem to be controlled by a man suffering from dementia. You will inform the board that the organization faces collapse, disgrace, and various federal investigations and prosecutions unless painful corrective measures are taken immediately.

You have never met most members of the Executive Committee, and you doubt your Strategic Plan will make a glowing first impression. Your strategic plan will bluntly describe the board's comprehensive failure over the last four years. The board will be asked to immediately double their financial contributions to the organization. You will recommend that your support staff be terminated, and that your own salary be reduced by another 10%. The board will be asked to remove the 47th most powerful man in Washington from his long-held role as treasurer.

You will explain how the organization's chief fundraising event—its annual Benefit—is actually losing money, and you will list all the ways in which that can be remedied: mainly by increasing revenue and reducing expense, which is basically the only management trick you've gleaned in these many years on Earth. You will ask the board to release its weirdly expensive meeting planner, Kathy Apple, a chain-smoking, dog-loving witch who seems to have cast some sort of dangerous hex upon one of the wealthiest women in the civilized world.

You wonder what font you should use for the headers. You format your bullet points, eliminate your weak verbs, and reduce modifiers. You insert charts, tables, pie charts, and bar graphs. You craft an argument so compelling a child could understand it, explaining causes, walking the board through the likely phases in this debacle, each one nastier than the last.

You revise. You copy edit. You mark as confidential and you hit send.

An hour after you send this document you receive a phone call from one of the members of the Executive Committee, Jess Abernathy. Jess Abernathy is one of the authors on the board. She wrote a bunch of crime novels in the late '70s that were turned into a movie called *Hoolihan*. You enjoyed this movie as a child, mostly because the lead character was a busty, morally ambiguous homicide cop on the South Side of Chicago who wasn't afraid to use sex to get information. You didn't really know whose side Hoolihan was on until the end, when she shot her drug-dealer lover three times in the face. There was no *Hoolihan 2*.

"John?" she asks. "You mind if I call you John?"

"Not at all," you say.

"Listen, I just happened to be sitting here when your report came through. I read that fucking thing in twenty minutes. Hilarious."

"I'm glad you—"

"I've been telling these pricks for years it's not that fucking complicated. All they want to do is sit around at their fancy parties and go to the Vineyard. Any one of 'em could write a check and solve the problem in ten minutes. I put up with it to the extent it helps me do what I do. Some of us are trying to make a difference with this thing, believe it or not. What are you doing for lunch?"

You meet Jess Abernathy in Anacostia. When you write grant proposals describing Quill & Pad's charitable efforts in this region, you describe Anacostia as "a historically underserved population." What you mean by "historically underserved population" is "poor and black." Quill & Pad's stated charitable purpose is to encourage reading among children. It fulfills this mission principally through its DC Books Program. Quill & Pad buys books for these kids, and sometimes famous authors come and visit these communities: their schools, their churches, their youth detention homes, their teenage mom support groups, and their jails.

You're given an address and there's a spot right outside. There's plenty of parking in Anacostia, and here your beat-up Volkswagen is a luxury automobile, surrounded by rusted out clunkers, several of which have giant yellow boots on the wheels. The roads haven't been paved in years. There's still a bit of a small-town look to the street, actually, with old stores and local bars, some of which are burnt out or boarded up. Thick, powerful weeds grow through warped sidewalks, up leaning chain-link fences. It's a Tuesday morning and twelve-year-old kids are running around the street. They should be in school. Perhaps you should not have worn your suit. Perhaps you should not take your leather laptop bag with you. Perhaps you should get in your car and drive away.

"Are you John?" a woman asks, and you're face-to-face with Jess Abernathy, an obese, grey-haired woman wearing a light purple sweat suit. The years have not been kind to Jess Abernathy. Her unkempt, thin hair falls around her broad shoulders. Her nose is pink and thick, and her blotchy skin is mapped with burst blood vessels. She's smoking. When she is not smoking she is thinking about smoking. She extends her hand to you, and you take it. She nods to the establishment behind her, a squat red brick building with no windows, no signs, and a metal door sprayed with graffiti.

She pushes the metal door open and inside it's a small bar, with a few wooden tables and mismatched chairs. There's a pinball machine in the corner (*Terminator 2*) and a couple people at the bar; thin, older black gentlemen who look like they've grown out of the red bar stools like fungus.

"Thanks for dressing up," she says, sitting down at one of

the tables. There are paper menus. "I wouldn't suggest the tuna tartar."

"Thanks for meeting me, Ms. Abernathy."

"Jess, please. Jess. And are you kidding? Pleasure's mine. I've been waiting ten years for someone like you."

A sleepy-looking waitress brings Jess Abernathy a rather large glass of whiskey, which as far as you know Jess didn't order. The waitress asks if you're ready to order.

"Maybe allow me, John. We'll take a couple half-smokes, Tanisha. You want anything to drink?"

"No, thanks."

The waitress nods, doesn't write anything down, and disappears behind a dirty kitchen door.

"So they tell me you're from Chicago."

"I am."

"You know I worked in Chicago for years, right?"

"I do. I'm a big fan of *Hoolihan*."

"Yeah? You seem a little young for all that."

"I was a kid when the movie came out on video."

"Ah, well, Jesus, the movie," she laughs, taking a belt, lighting another cigarette. "You know they lost fifteen million dollars on that movie? And that's back when fifteen million was a lot of money."

"I didn't know that."

"That was it for ole Cat Hoolihan. But that was back when you could actually make a living writing books. They were gonna do a TV show before that but I had to be such a big shot. I was too good for TV. TV's where the real money is, you know. Especially for writers."

She slaps her forehead, as if to suggest she's an idiot.

"Then the market crash, Jesus, I'll tell you something, John, it doesn't matter who you are. Life's gonna give you some swift kicks in the ass. I should've stayed on the force. Don't get me wrong, I'm doing okay, but in case you haven't noticed, I'm not like Alice Cavanaugh-Williams.

"I don't wanna offend you; I don't mean any offense. But they're all just a bunch of starfuckers. You know that, don't you? All they want is to get Salman Rushdie in their fucking living rooms so they can show 'em off to their friends. That's all you gotta know about that crowd. Christ almighty and this fucking Benefit. Stay as far away from that as you can. Wait until they do the seating chart. My God. Problem is, they don't think like you and me. In case you haven't figured that out yet. They're different. They really are. It took me a long time to understand that about this town. Chicago, you know, even the rich people in Chicago, they work. Here everybody just runs around screaming at each other. And in Chicago—look, there's not rich there like there's rich out here. This is a different kind of rich. You know what I mean?"

"I think so," you smile. Finally somebody you like.

"And they're all just so goddamned *dumb*. Not a one of 'em could add two and two together. Because they don't care. It doesn't mean anything to them. I saw, what did you say, we're a million in the hole?"

"Yes," you say. "Well, more like eight or nine in the hole."

She whistles. "I bet you're wishing you never came here."

"There have been days, yes,"

"Well listen," she says. "I could never figure it out. It's just math, right? I'd get these reports that didn't make any sense to me. I'd ask questions, and then they'd hand me to that Albert guy, and he's—well I don't know if you've met him, but he's not playing with a full deck. Nice guy. Needs to be in a home, not managing a hedge fund. But whatever, it is what it is. I figure, well, they're rich, if they don't care, I don't care. But listen, me? I'm here to help you. That's how I see my role. But I don't do these dinner parties. I'll go to whatever board meeting you want me to, say whatever you need me to, and you might not think it, but I clean up real good. They respect me. And they know, the writers, they come to their cocktail hours because *I* ask them. I still got some pull. I know people in that world. They don't give a shit about Alice Cavanaugh-Williams. I'll go in and talk about all the poor children. I know how to say things to these people. I assume you know they wanna fire you."

"Yes," you nod. "Well. I had a feeling,"

"Your little report's probably not gonna make it harder for 'em," she says. "And what did you do to piss off Kathy Apple?"

"I don't know, really," you say. "I met with her. I asked her what she does for half-a-million dollars."

"Ha!" Jess laughs, slapping her hand on the table so hard it shakes. "What did she say?"

"Nothing. I guess I just don't get it," you say. "Who is Kathy Apple?"

"I've been asking that same question for fifteen years. She does the seating chart, and for that, we pay her half-a-million bucks a year. You know how much good you could do down here with half-a-million bucks? You know how far that goes in a place like this?"

"But why? Why do they pay her so much?"

She shrugs, blows a long plume of smoke.

"Why does anybody do anything? Only thing I know in life is that there are really only two reasons people do anything, really. Sex and food. And Alice is a skinny bitch. You met Kathy Apple? At first I thought they might be lesbians, the two of them, the way Alice protects her. Which wouldn't matter to me one bit. It would explain a lot. But then I was thinking even if Alice was a dyke—that would just seem, I don't know—*gauche*— to someone like her, to slum it with a plebeian like Kathy Apple.

It's dirty. It's *untoward*. They don't breed outside their class you know. That's why they got all these head problems. The rich. It's all the inbreeding. Everybody's second cousins twice removed, everybody's known each other since they were six months old. But who knows what it's all about. Kathy Apple—she gets around this town. You wouldn't think it to look at her, but she knows everybody. And not just the people up top, but *aaalllll* those people just right below the top. The bureaucrats. The undersecretaries and all those people. All those boring people you hear on C-Span, the anonymous bald fuckers they never get rid of, the people who actually get shit done. Presidents come and go, those guys stay there *forever*. She's like J. Edgar Hoover over there. So maybe she knows something about Miss Cavanaugh-Williams. Has to. And that's why Alice is here. She gives a bunch of money to Quill & Pad, and Quill & Pad turns around and gives the money to Kathy Apple, and nobody's the wiser, and whatever's left over goes to the kids."

"There's not anything left over," you say. "Actually, the education program is underwriting the benefit."

"Don't I know it," Jess says.

The waitress brings your half smokes in red plastic baskets lined with wax paper. It looks like a steaming pile of diarrhea on a hot dog bun, but it smells amazing, like chili powder, onion, and sausage. Jess reassures you.

"Like anything decent in this town it seems disgusting at first, but it looks better and better as time goes on," she says, digging in, and then, with her mouth full, chili dribbling down her chin, "Listen, after lunch I'll take you down to see some of the kids. Get your spirits up."

*

You ride in Jess's white van down potholed streets, through intersections without working traffic lights, past gas stations and currency exchanges promising payday advances, and finally you arrive at Lincoln High School, a huge building that looks like it might be a prison. There are very few windows at Lincoln High School. The sidewalk out front is broad and cracked, and when you walk up the steps to the front door, a security guard greets you and frisks you with a wand.

"You're good," he says, waving you inside.

Inside there are three metal detectors, conveyor belts, more security guards. Like at the airport.

"You don't have to take off your shoes," one of the guards says. There's a police dog there, too.

"I'm from Quill & Pad," Jess says to one of the guards. "I'm here to drop off some books for the kids?"

"Oh yeah," the guard says, checking a clipboard. "Abernathy. Q&P. This you?"

"That's me."

"Sign here," the guard says. A bell rings and suddenly the hallway behind the security checkpoint is filled with kids. You notice a public service poster hanging on the wall. It shows a smiling black doctor with a needle. Underneath him it reads, "Be Smart. Get Vaccinated." Above the poster there's a security camera moving like a metronome.

"You can go 'head and bring 'em around back to the loading bay. Chuck'll meet you back there."

"Thanks," Jess says, and you follow her back to the van.

"Lotta security," you say.

"Three kids got shot here last year," she says. "But it's just like the airport. It's stupid to spend all this money. I guess it makes people feel better, but they want to get a gun in they'll find a way. It's a high school for Christ's sake."

You drive around back to the loading dock, where you're met by Chuck, a thick, clean-cut Latino man wearing a janitor's uniform. He holds a metal security door open.

"Just roll 'em on up, Jess," he says, motioning to a ramp. You follow Jess around back of her van and open it up, and there's a metal book cart, the kind you see at a library, wrapped round with bungee cords and secured to the wall. The van is filled with cardboard boxes overflowing with new books. Not textbooks, but bestsellers, poetry books, history books, biographies, political books. All hardcover. All pristine.

"You wanna leave your jacket in the front seat?"

＊

Once you've brought the books inside the gymnasium, you're met by a group of teachers. There are two kinds of teachers. They are either very-young or very-old. Mostly women, but there's a few men. There are more white teachers in the younger crowd, and they're dressed impeccably. They look eager, confident, and out of place. The older teachers are dressed more casually, and they look tired, beaten up. The older teachers are exclusively African American. Jess talks with a couple of them while the kids walk around the books eagerly. They browse in small, random groups, all assigned by some unknown mechanism.

"John, you met Gloria Davis?" Jess asks, motioning you over to the group. "Gloria's the English Chair here at Lincoln. John's the new Executive Director over at Quill & Pad."

Gloria's an attractive older woman wearing a red dress and long turquoise jewelry. She smiles broadly and shakes your hand vigorously with both of her hands.

"Thanks so much for doing this," she says.

"I didn't do anything," you say.

"John's our fundraising guy," Jess says, giving you a slight punch on the shoulder. "He puts up with a lotta BS to get us these books."

"Well we appreciate everything you do," Gloria says.

You're not sure what to say. But you are impressed by both what's available and what the kids pick out. There's no light reading there. You don't know how these books got here. You haven't signed a check for any of them. But there are hundreds and hundreds of them, all new, all current. There are graphic novels, too, kids' books, anthologies, even some very nice Modern Library editions of Langston Hughes, H.P. Lovecraft, and Wallace Stevens.

A tall, lanky kid with a baggy sweatshirt and huge headphones wanders around the books looking for something. Jess calls out to him.

"Michael," she says, waving him over.

The kid saunters over to Jess as she takes something out of her large handbag. It's a beautiful, hardcover edition of Raymond Chandler's *The Big Sleep*. You're not sure but you think it might be a first edition. She hands it to him.

Michael takes the book and stares at the cover.

"Ms. Davis says you really liked *The Maltese Flacon*?"

The kid nods, but does not look her in the eye. He just stares down at the book, his headphones still on.

"Michael, take off your headphones when Miss Abernathy is talking," Gloria says.

The kid takes off his headphones and shrugs.

"Sorry," he says. You can barely hear him.

"Ah, don't worry about it. If you liked *The Maltese Falcon* I think you'll like this one. This is a guy named Raymond Chandler. This guy was a real badass. He was a pilot in the Royal Air Force during World War II. He had a bit of a drinking problem. Ms. Davis says you're reading William Faulkner in class?"

The kid nods.

"How do you like Faulkner?"

He shrugs.

"We're having a hard time with Faulkner," Ms. Davis says.

"Yeah well, me too. I always had a hard time with Faulkner," Jess says, tapping the book. "You'll like this better. After this book was published, William Faulkner was hired to write the movie."

The kid looks up.

"There's a movie?"

"Yeah there's a famous movie for this one, just like *The Maltese Falcon*. Same actor and everything. And at the time, this guy—Chandler—he was so pissed off that Faulkner got hired to write the movie. And Faulkner read this book, and he couldn't figure out one of the murders. There's a guy in the book who gets killed and Faulkner couldn't tell who did it. So he called Chandler up and he asked him, he said, 'Hey, Chandler, I read this *Big Sleep* and I can't figure out who killed this guy,' and Chandler, who was probably drunk—well, let's be honest, they were probably both drunk—Chandler says to William Faulkner, 'Well they're paying you to write the g-damned movie, you figure it out.'"

He laughs.

"Movie's great. But the book's better. You'll like it. Trust me."

"A'right," Michael says. "Thanks Miss Abernathy."

"I got you this, too," she says, pulling out a sheet of stapled Xeroxes. "Later in his life, William Faulkner tried to write stories like Raymond Chandler. Detective stories, I mean. He really respected Chandler, even though Chandler hated him. Faulkner got all the praise and people thought this guy Chandler was a real hack. But Faulkner knew better. He had good taste. So try this out and see what you think. Then try going back to the Faulkner book you're reading in class. He's an acquired taste."

"Thanks," he says casually, holding the book up. "Yeah, thanks."

*

After you pack up the remaining books, you get back in the van and Jess drives you back to your car.

"You know, it's not really all that complicated," she says, lighting up a cigarette. "Now they're going to elect a new president. Everybody's gonna talk about education reform. Again. Then somebody will come up with some new fucking system all these poor teachers have to learn. Nobody will actually talk to any teachers, mind you. They'll just give 'em a whole set of new tests. New standards. Tell Ms. Davis in there that if her kids aren't up to the same level as the spoiled brats at Sidwell Academy they're gonna shut the place down and fire her. All this time and money wasted, and nobody ever just goes to these places and *gives these kids a goddamned book*. Something that's theirs. Something they own, something private that belongs to them and them only. You want to get kids to read? You think Michael in there's got a goddamned interest in William Faulkner? Why the hell would they make 'em read *The Sound and the Fury?* Some drunk white Southerner from 1935? What the hell does he have in common with that? He's not gonna read that. *I'm* not gonna read that. You look like a reader. You got *Absalom, Absalom!* sitting on the back of your toilet? First you have to *engage* them, you have to just get them *willing* to learn, willing to read. That kid Michael? He's smart as a whip. He's got the talent, too, he just knows how to put words together. Doesn't say much, but he's got the ear, and you can't teach that. But he's not gonna sit down and read the fucking modernists unless you come at it sideways."

"Where did you get the books?"

"I got arrangements with the publishers, the bookstores, they give me a good deal. Sometimes they send me remainders. I'm coordinating most of it out of my house. Do one school a week. Then I pay up front for everything and I send you the invoice for the books once a quarter. It's not cheap, but it's not like we're talking about a million dollars, either. All told I think we spend sixty, seventy grand a year doing this. Not counting my time or gas or anything. But that's on me."

"That's cheap."

"Compared to all the other shit we do, you're goddamned right it's cheap. So when I read we're wasting this money on Kathy Apple and we're spending a million bucks on a goddamned benefit that's not raising any money, you bet I'm pissed off."

"Have you thought about a used book drive or anything?"

"No," she says, shaking her head. "No used books. That's all these kids ever get. Beat up, second-hand crap. Lot of those kids have never even been inside a library, let alone a bookstore. All they get is junk. Junk clothes, junk food, junk schools, junk life. I don't wanna give them more junk. I wanna give them something *new*—show them there's a different world out there, and it's endless, and you can get there pretty cheap, long as you're willing to put in the reading. No. They get new books nobody's ever read or there's no point in me doing it."

"Except when it comes to *The Big Sleep*."

"Well," she smiles. "That kid's a different story."

CYCLES AND JOURNEYS

Dr. Greenspan explains the cycle to you. You will need to produce another specimen. After this, the entire cycle takes about 4-7 weeks. Your wife will continue her birth control medication and then start on hormone treatment. Something about suppression. You are trying to follow all of it. He writes it down on a nice flow chart for you to understand. At one point you will have to give Liesl a Trigger Shot.

"This is normally administered in the buttocks," he explains.

The Lupron will need to be refrigerated. Your insurance may cover some of the medications, but you will see Dawn in billing to go through all of that.

The flow chart is quite linear. You are taking notes. Liesl is taking notes. At some point you will have to give the Trigger Shot. The timing of this shot is very important. It must be administered within a small time frame, which is determined by Liesl's cycle. He shows you how to administer the Trigger Shot. You practice on a small pillow.

"Just flick the wrist. Just like this," he says, helping you.

You flick the syringe down into the pillow.

"Make sure you inject the contents in one slow, fluid motion. Don't stop. It should be a 5-7 count."

You plunge the back of the syringe down with your thumb, counting aloud.

"You're going to encounter some resistance about halfway through the trigger shot. That's perfectly normal, keep going, you're doing great."

You empty the syringe and Dr. Greenspan smiles.

"Excellent. Good job."

He explains the theory of what they're doing. They're taking control of Liesl's cycle. There will be suppression, stimulation, the trigger, and then a harvest. Post-harvest there will be insemination. Cultivation. Implantation.

"I want you to be realistic," Dr. Greenspan says. "There is no guarantee. There is never a guarantee. And there are risks associated."

You don't have any risks. Your big risk is missing the cup. But Liesl might miscarry. Liesl might get an infection.

"We try to avoid multiple pregnancies at Shared Promise," he says.

Also something called hyperstimulation.

"It's a bit of a misnomer because all IVF patients undergo hyperstimulation," Dr. Greenspan shrugs.

But sometimes it gets out of control. Sometimes it's more serious. Sometimes you get fluid buildup and infection and you might have to be hospitalized and have your ovaries removed.

"But I don't want to scare you," he says.

*

Dawn in billing does not have a medical degree. Dawn's good with spreadsheets. She doesn't smile as much as everyone else at Shared Promise. She has a copy of your credit report and your insurance policies. She reads credit reports and health insurance policies for a living. She has some good news and some bad news. But mostly bad news.

She gives you another flowchart showing how much money you'll need at various points. She lines it up next to the one Dr. Greenspan gave you. You get the feeling she does this a lot. You get the feeling that there has been a meeting to talk about how to line up the flowcharts after consultation with the doctor.

She has a few questions. Do you own a car? What is outstanding on the loan? How much equity do you have in your home? Do you have student loans? Can you tell me about any other net assets? Do you have a 401K plan? How much is in your savings account? What is your gross pay? Might we get copies of your last three tax returns? How long have you been employed at Quill & Pad? Who should she call to verify employment? Did you bring your most recent paystub? Would you like to apply for financing?

It's all part of your conception journey.

HIVES

Over the weekend you break out in hives. This has never happened to you before. At least you think they're hives. You don't know what they are. You're having some kind of reaction. They itch like hell. Between Thursday night and Saturday morning they spread from the tops of your feet all the way up your legs. At first they start out like red splotches, and then they quickly change to brownish-red scales about three inches in diameter. The ones on the back of your knees are the real killers. Suddenly you can't bend your legs or the scabs keep cracking and bleeding, and so you have to walk with your legs straightened, shuffling around like the tin man from room to room. You buy gauze pads and tape, and they help for as long as they stay on. But they quickly slide off the ones at your joints. Now they don't itch, they just hurt. It's a constant, chronic pain, all over your body, and you're amazed at how symmetrical they are. They pop up in the exact same place on each side of your body.

"You need to see somebody," Liesl advises. And this time, you take her advice.

Your doc can see you at 11:30, so you roll on over there

with your weeping hives, covered in so many bandages and gauze you might as well be the Invisible Man. *Even the moon is frightened of you!*

The doctor's name is Dr. Krauss. He's a kindly old German fellow with a thick grey beard and tiny glasses. He reminds you of Santa Claus.

Once again you find yourself sitting on an examination table with your pants down. Dr. Krauss is bending in front of you, adjusting his glasses. He doesn't know what to make of your condition.

"Are you allergic to anything?"

"Not that I'm aware of."

"Have you changed detergents recently?"

"No."

"Eat anything out of the ordinary? Anything unusual, outside your own diet? Shellfish?"

"No," then you pause. "Wait. I did have a half-smoke a couple days ago."

"What is this 'half smoke'?"

"It's like a hot dog. A sausage. With chili on top."

"When did you eat this?"

"Two days ago. Thursday."

"And it started after that?"

"I guess. The next day. I woke up Friday and I was itchy all over. Am I allergic to sausage?"

"I would be quite surprised if sausage was the culprit," he says, tipping his glasses. "But I don't know what this is. The half smoke. Have you had sausage before? Chili?"

"Yes."

"But never any adverse reaction?"

"No. I love chili."

"Have you been camping recently; did you walk in any tall

grass?"

"No."

"Have you been in any strange environments? Any place outside your normal habitat?"

"No. Well. Yes, I went to a school in Anacostia. In DC"

"A school?"

"A high school."

"Well. Something in your environment has triggered this," he says. "You're having a systemic autoimmune response."

"Like an allergic reaction?"

"I only hesitate to say yes because these don't present like traditional hives," he says, and then, squatting down in front of you, he pokes at one of your scabs with some kind of metal pointer. It hurts. "It looks more like severe eczema or psoriasis, but I've never seen it so progressed in a person your age. Has this ever happened to you before?"

"No. What's that? What's eczema?"

"Have you been under any unusual stress lately?"

You start to respond, but then you just start crying. You try to stop it but you can't control yourself. You feel silly and out of control. You hold your hands up to your eyes to try to stop it, but you can't. You blubber incoherent sentences this poor man can't possibly follow about sperm, ghosts, and strategic plans. Jesus, what is wrong with you? Your grandmother had polio, for Christ's sake. What are you bitching about? Man up. *Man up*, you tell yourself, *stop complaining, stop blubbering in front of this stranger, you're acting like a crazy person.*

But you can't stop. Because you're weak. You apologize to the doctor for your weakness. You tell him that you have no money and you're about to have much less. You're hundreds of thousands of dollars in debt and you're trying to get yourself fired. But you understand the problem now. The *real* problem. The real problem is you've always been weak. That's why God hates you. God hates weaklings and cowards. That's why you're to be rubbed out of the universe. Because you're a failure, and you were born a failure. It's not surprising that you fail at everything. You're failing in your marriage. You're failing in your job. You're failing as a man. Now Liesl has to take on all the risks, and you have to sit back and let her. And now you're failing in front of Dr. Krauss, with your weeping weak skin and your breakdown.

The doctor listens to you patiently, nodding, listening, and finally, when you get some marginal control of yourself, he puts his gentle German Santa hand on your shoulder. He seems so calm and normal. He's aware this sort of thing has happened before.

"So today I'm going to go ahead and give you a prescription for a topical steroid," he says. "But I'm also going to refer you to a dermatologist. And a psychiatrist."

POLITICS

.

It's cold and raining and you're waiting in your Volkswagen Golf in the circular driveway in front of Alice Cavanaugh-Williams's house. The driveway is brick. You're twenty minutes early for a meeting with a committee of strangers. At the conclusion of this meeting you are likely to be unemployed. You have no desire to wait in the sitting room.

You've parked in front of the statue of William Henry Cavanaugh, all six feet of him, a bronze American God covered in patina, pasted with late November leaves. Washington is beautiful in the fall. It's more honest. William Henry Cavanaugh still looks imposing, with his enormous sideburns and his commanding moustache, his hands on his hips, staring down Massachusetts Avenue like he owns the joint. At one point he did. At one point William Henry Cavanaugh commanded 2.4% of the total Gross Domestic Product of the United States. You read this statistic in the Pulitzer Prize-winning biography, which was full of grainy nineteenth century pictures of the man. The book told of his squalid upbringing in rural Ohio. His wealth was compared to that of Bill Gates, adjusted for inflation. Side by side, and at the peak of their fortunes, William Henry Cavanaugh was more than 900% richer than Bill Gates.

You imagine what you would do with such a fortune. It's hard to imagine. William Henry Cavanaugh didn't know what to do with it, and you imagine he was a much shrewder individual than you. Cavanaugh spent the later part of his life trying to give the money away, but found it much more difficult than he imagined it would be.

From *American Baron: The Life of William Henry Cavanaugh:*

A master of efficiency and vertical integration, Cavanaugh could not understand the inefficiency of philanthropic institutions, infected everywhere by good intentions and bad business practices. Cavanaugh sought to make social investments, and he expected tangible returns on his investment. Instead he found his charity squandered, and in some cases, even stolen. In 1893, Cavanaugh made a $100,000 gift to a supposed Pastor named Ernest Pisario, who claimed to be able to rehabilitate alcohol addiction in vagrants. Cavanaugh was mortified to discover that Pisario was neither a pastor nor a social reformer, but merely a slick huckster from Indiana who absconded with the money as soon as it was in hand. Despite numerous attempts to recover the funds, which Cavanaugh pursued to his death, Pisario was never found and the money never recovered.

Cavanaugh's lifelong press nemesis Ida Scanlon penned scathing press stories relishing in humiliating Cavanaugh for his foolish and misguided attempts at "world-fixing." Embarrassed, enraged, and genuinely humbled by the experience, Cavanaugh did what he did best: innovate.

"In my retirement from industry I have made sincere attempts to invest in sound philanthropic institutions. But since I have found that they do not presently exist, I shall need to create them."

Remarkably, the Pisario Scandal led to the establishment of the Cavanaugh Institute, which Cavanaugh established and ran until his death in 1903. The Institute was the Gates Foundation of its day, and even today, it remains one of the largest and most effective philanthropic institutions in the world.

You have applied for funding for Quill & Pad from the Cavanaugh Institute, as you have from dozens of foundations since you discovered your organization is on the brink of financial collapse. They were indeed efficient, responding within two weeks with a letter that began, "Thank you for your interest in the Cavanaugh Institute. Unfortunately…" You have since discovered that the Cavanaugh Institute is controlled by a separate warring faction of the Cavanaugh family. You think you might like the other part of the family, and you respect them for rejecting your application. That's what you would do if you were in charge of a billion bucks.

Despite that, and somewhat remarkably, in the last six weeks you've raised $250,000 of the $1 million you need to avoid bankruptcy, mostly in $5,000 and $10,000 chunks from small foundations and corporations. This you would count as a small miracle, if you weren't also convinced that the easy work was now done. You might be able to cobble together another $50,000 or $100,000, but that would still leave you hundreds of thousands short of your needs. The board is reluctant to increase their donations, and in reality, there are really only two individuals on the board who have the kind of money you need: one is trying to fire you, and the other is insane.

You're smoking a cigarette. You haven't smoked in years, but you've decided to take it up again. Smoking is terrible for your sperm production, or so sayeth one of the many experts you've consulted, maybe the fertility doc, the psychiatrist, the internist, the dermatologist, or the allergist—the most recent and exciting addition to your growing health care team. The allergist has posited that the mess of ulcerous legions that have suddenly erupted on your body might stem from a dangerous mold growing in your home.

"But I think we should do a biopsy to be on the safe side."

Time for your meeting!

*

You have come to discuss various charts and bullet points, which you have prepared and disseminated in PDF format. You have brought printed copies. One of Alice Cavanaugh-Williams' minority servants helps you distribute them around the table.

The white sitting room you previously spent so much time in has been arranged like a conference room. Someone has brought in a very long table to accommodate more than a dozen guests. The table weighs several hundred pounds. It is thick mahogany. It looks like it once sat in parliament, as do the ornate wooden chairs, which are filled by people you've never met before. Alice Cavanaugh-Williams sits at the head of the table, forcing you to stand awkwardly from the middle as you deliver your remarks. The only other people you recognize are Algernon Albert and his nurse/receptionist Cindy, and Jess Abernathy, who has indeed cleaned up for the event. Everyone looks very serious as they flip through your report.

"John's going to speak for a few minutes," Alice says. "And then I'd like to put a motion before the committee."

"Thank you," you say, standing up. "I hope everyone's had a chance to review the documents I sent last week. If you turn to page five, you'll find two charts that demonstrate the core problem."

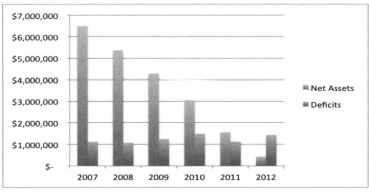

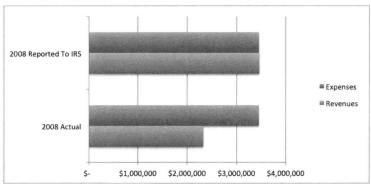

To you, these charts are horrific, but they have apparently not made much of an impression on the committee. You have tried to keep the charts as simple as possible, to explain the problem in a clear voice to six-year-olds. You want to distance yourself from the board's decisions and express alarm over the state of the organization's finances and past behaviors. You speak loudly and you stand your ground.

You tell the board you have discovered improprieties and you are now bringing them to the attention of the board, which is your legal obligation.

"You also have an obligation in all this," you say directly.

You deliver your remarks with a smile on your face, looking each board member in the eye as you do. When you are finished, Algernon Albert raises his hand.

"Yes. Albert." Alice says peevishly.

"Are we properly insured?" he asks, surprisingly incisive.

"Yes and no," you say. "This body—the board of directors—is insured against liability by the organization's Directors and Officers policy."

Jess raises her hand.

"I'm sorry, what is that?" she asks.

"The Directors and Officers policy—it's an insurance policy that protects the officers of the corporation from liability and prosecution, in the event of any lawsuits. Except the board must demonstrate that they have exercised due care in their fiduciary capacity. I would tell you quite honestly you haven't."

"Excuse me?" Alice chimes in.

"I said you have not exercised due care and oversight," you say louder. "From a legal perspective. Or that argument could be made rather convincingly. I'd presume that, given the material misstatements and the amount of time this has been going on, a good case could be made that the policy might not cover the trustees should anything happen. You are responsible."

Algernon adjusts his glasses and leans in, flipping through your report. You see that the entire board is looking at him, waiting for him to speak.

"So what you're saying is, we're on the hook," he smiles, leans back in his chair, and then he winks at you.

"Uh. Yes sir. That's right, sir."

"Well. We're on the hook," he nods, holding his hands up.

"And so far, our 'Executive' has failed to raise the money we need," Alice says. "We've never had this problem before."

"He's only been here two months, Alice," Jess says.

"And after all that time he asks members of this board to... to do what, exactly? Am I supposed to sit here and be insulted?"

"I'm not trying to insult you," you explain. "I'm sorry if it appears that way. I have an obligation to tell you—"

"Why don't you just raise some money?" Alice asks.

"Well," you say. "I have already raised an additional $250,000 in new revenues, and I've sent out dozens of grant applications and appeals. But you have to understand the magnitude of this situation, and the time we have to solve it. Many of these funding decisions won't be made for months. And you also have to understand, I cannot, knowing what I know, misrepresent our financial position to potential funders. That would be in violation of *my* fiduciary obligation. I can dress it up, I can avoid the conversation, but if asked, I can't lie. Funders are sophisticated. Most of them will ask for several years of financial data. They're not going to look at deficits like this and be excited to invest. Would you invest in an enterprise that was operating a 40% budget deficit year over year? It appears irresponsible. It looks like bad management."

"I think it's quite clear there's bad management," Alice snaps.

"Well what about expenses?" Jess adds. "I mean, maybe it's time we talk about Kathy Apple..."

"Kathy..." Alice starts, flabbergasted and offended. "I will not let you run your personal vendetta against Kathy Apple in my home. Kathy Apple has nothing to do with this. We are getting a steal with her. A steal. We are lucky to live in the same world as Kathy Apple! She would never have let this happen. Never! Everyone here knows how crucial she is. She fills the tables. She does everything for this event. There wouldn't be a Quill & Pad without Kathy Apple."

"There may not be one *with* her," Jess says.

"I will not be part of this organization without Kathy Apple. I have a motion."

"Alice," Jess says, shaking her head.

"I have a motion! These problems all started when we hired our current Executive Director. I think you all know how I felt about that decision, and now I think it's crystal clear why I had reservations. We have never, ever been in this kind of position before. Ever. Certainly Vanessa would not have let this happen. I voiced my concern then, and I have been patient, but for the sake of Quill & Pad, an organization that I have loved and supported for more than thirty years, I can no longer in good conscience support this Executive. I move that we replace this Executive Director immediately."

"Really, Alice?" Jess asks. "Really? You're going to do this right in front of him? He's standing right there!"

"I have a motion on the table! I have a motion! Albert, would you please second?"

And you're excited. You smile.

Come on. Please fire me. Please.

Suddenly Algernon starts coughing violently. Cindy, his nurse/receptionist, shoots up quickly and runs over to him and pats his back. He waves her off and stands up slowly, bracing himself on the hard wood table.

"Mr. Albert, do you need some water?" Cindy asks. "Can somebody get him some water?"

"Akkkk!" he hacks and coughs, Cindy patting him on the back, and you're about to call an ambulance when he appears to vomit something into his cupped hand. Then he holds it up and shows it to Cindy.

"Well, it's a tooth!" he says, and he holds it up for the rest of the Executive Committee to see. "Would you look at that?"

Except it doesn't look like a tooth. It looks like something that used to be a tooth, but has been soaked for a thousand years in black coffee. It's a tiny, grey nub of a tooth, a former molar, and once Albert's done showing it off, he pulls his wallet from his back pocket and tucks it in there, presumably for the tooth fairy.

Then he sits back down.

"Do we need to have a fundraiser?" he asks, smiling. "Let's have a fundraiser!"

WAIVERS

At 5:30 on Friday morning you're lying in a hospital bed. The Urologist hands you a stack of papers the size of a telephone book. These papers describe all the things that can happen to you when someone slices open your scrotum and physically alters the blood vessels feeding your testicles. The list of potential problems has not really changed since your first consultation with the Urologist, but you are impressed by the legal protections afforded to doctors. Clearly they've thought things through.

You've been thinking a lot about legal liability since you weren't fired as Executive Director of Quill & Pad. Although, if you're going to be a stickler for Robert's Rules of Order, technically speaking, there's still a motion on the table. Nevertheless, it doesn't seem likely you're going to be removed from your position just yet. You're not sure this is a good thing for you. But right now you need to get your balls cut open.

"And sign here, please," the nurse says, handing you another ten-page packet and pointing to a line.

"What does this one say?"

"This concerns the anesthesia," the nurse says. "You'll

be having general anesthesia today. You've indicated you're not allergic, to your knowledge, to the anesthesia. In rare cases, anesthesia can cause serious side effects."

All day side effects and rare cases have been laid out for you, mostly describing the same set of scenarios. There are about a thousand different potential outcomes, ranging from mild irritation to death. No one must be held accountable.

You nod and sign on the tenth page, and you are handed another long document to read and sign. Your Directors and Officers policy is two pages long. You have avoided being fired but now you're the man on the letterhead, and you're a million dollars in the red. But don't worry. An insane, tooth-dispensing codger has volunteered to throw a fundraiser for you.

You sign and sign and sign, until finally you're done and you're left alone with Liesl, who sits in a plastic chair beside your bed. She squeezes your hand. Why are you thinking about all that now? You're lying in a hospital bed wearing a loosely-tied paper robe. Liesl is crying. Not full on. She's wiping a tear from her cheek.

"Why are you crying?" you ask.

She smiles, squeezes.

"I love you," she says, wiping away her long blond hair from her face. As you lie there, you realize how beautiful she is. You don't notice it as much as you used to. As much as you should. Her high cheek bones, her smile. Nobody smiles like your wife. You've been a real asshole to Liesl.

"I've been a real asshole," you say, but you're not really saying it to her. You turn to face the curtains surrounding you. God, you've been an asshole. Man, you've been self-centered. Man, you've been about the biggest prick you can be to the one person in this whole mess who actually gives a shit about you. "You don't deserve this. I want a baby, you know."

"I know," she says.

"I'm sorry I can't just give you one. Like a normal person," you say, squeezing her hand. "I wish I was normal."

Then you feel yourself starting to cry. But you don't want to cry, especially not here, in this room. "This totally isn't going to work is it?"

She laughs, a bittersweet half-cry/half-laugh.

"It might work," she shrugs.

"No," you say, and you know you're telling yourself the truth. "This is not going to work. I wonder how much this is going to cost?"

"The insurance will cover it."

"No, I know, but—I wonder how much he's gonna charge for doing this. It's kind of crazy. To pay someone to cut open your balls."

"Well, at least your balls won't shrink," she says.

"That is a plus. I don't think they can get much smaller."

"John. Don't say that," she says, squeezing.

"I'm sorry, Liesl. I'm really sorry."

"It's okay. We're gonna be okay."

"Talk about something else. To distract me."

"What should I talk about?"

"I don't know…anything."

"Uh, well…they moved the English department to the trailers."

"The trailers?"

"I'm sorry. The *learning cottages*. That's what they're calling them. The learning cottages. But they're trailers."

"Why?"

"There's asbestos in the ceiling."

"That's great."

"No shit. You should see the Math and Science classrooms,

though. They redid them last year. It's like being in a hotel over there. The learning cottages suck. They don't even have bathrooms. The rooms are ten feet wide. I have thirty-five kids who barely fit in there, and if one of them has to pee, they have to walk outside and across campus."

"That sounds terrible."

"It's not so bad," she says, squeezing your hand. "Everything's gonna be fine, John."

Yes. It's all going to be fine. Why are you worried? It's all routine. You should be out of here in three hours. The procedure itself will only take about twenty minutes. Why, you'll be able to resume work in a day or two! There will be some slight swelling in your scrotum, obviously. Some mild discomfort. But within a week you should be able to resume your normal activities. No weightlifting for a month.

You really should lift more weights.

You should see the Colosseum.

You should learn Chinese.

The doctor throws back the curtain.

PART FOUR

REESE WITHERSPOON

You're lying on the couch with a bag of frozen peas on your balls and your legs spread apart. You're extremely uncomfortable. There are long, oval bruises on both of your inner thighs and you're not sure how they got there. Your scrotum is the size of a softball. Sunlight is streaming through the cheap curtains in your living room. Why can't it be cloudy today?

You're watching a Reese Witherspoon movie on basic cable. You'd change the channel but you're strangely engaged in the plot. Will they reconcile? Will she realize that she needs to change her ways and give up her ambitions to please her man? Life is give and take.

Perhaps it's the painkillers. You don't feel funny but Liesl has informed you that you're not acting like yourself. You feel like yourself. You think you're thinking clearly.

It's 11:00 a.m. and you're eating lime sherbet. Goddamn, you love lime sherbet. The surgery went just fine, and your testicles are no longer atrophying. Judging by the swelling they might be expanding on a cosmic scale. But there are certain foods you want to avoid over the next week. You need to have a bowel-friendly diet. No more pumpkin seeds! A strenuous bowel movement could rip the sutures.

"And we don't want that!" the Urologist said, patting you on the shoulder.

Your phone is ringing.

"Don't get that," Liesl says, but it's a Thursday, and if you don't get it, who will? "Don't answer that!"

Why is she trying to stop you?

"Don't try to stop me!" you warn Liesl. "John McManus," you say confidently.

"We need Hector Siffuentes' flight information."

"Hello Kathy," you say, pausing your movie.

There's a pause on the other end.

"Well?"

"He hasn't made his flight arrangements yet."

"Well why not? I thought you were all trying to save money now. Cut corners. Are you going to wait until the last minute? Flight prices go up."

"The world will still keep turning."

"What are you talking about? And why does the Ritz have two adjoining suites for him?"

"He needs one for his ghost."

"Are you drunk?"

"No. I'm actually fairly serious. He has a ghost and he won't come without a room."

"This is outrageous! I'm getting told to cut corners and you're reserving suites at the Ritz for ghosts?!"

"Yes. Hey. Have you seen *Sweet Home Alabama?* Whatever happened to this guy? He has the bluest eyes."

"This isn't over!"

She hangs up.

"Who was that?" Liesl asks. "Why did you get the phone?"

"Whatever happened to this guy from *Sweet Home Alabama?* The glassblower?"

"Babe, I love you, but seriously—you shouldn't be answering the phone. You have to trust me. You shouldn't be talking to anyone right now."

"Fucking Hollywood. They'll chew you up and spit you out!"

Then you take a huge spoonful of lime sherbet.

*

Ten hours later you're feeling much better, about to go to sleep, when your phone starts lighting up. Email after email, ping ping ping. You pick it up and see an email chain forming. Kathy Apple has sent an email. Never in all her years has she been so disgraced and humiliated, never has she been treated with more discourtesy, never has she considered simply leaving Quill & Pad behind.

"I have such fond memories of all those wonderful authors on our stages," she waxes. "And in the old days, with Albert and Alice on the Vineyard, those beautiful summer evenings—and yet even the slightest sense of self-respect or decency would cry out for some accommodation."

A modicum of respect. A simple thank you. Recognition.

Board members are flying out of the woodwork, begging her to stay on, apologizing for any miscommunication, issuing statements of support, promising to get to the bottom of this mess.

Ping.

Ping.

Ping.

"Don't answer," Liesl says.

"But…"

"No!" Liesl says, snatching your phone. "No. That's it. No."

"You don't understand…"

"John, you had surgery this morning. This morning. What is wrong with you? You shouldn't be talking to anyone."

"I'm fine."

"You're not fine," she says, and she holds up your phone. "Whatever this is, it's not important. It can wait."

"You don't understand! They have to fire me!"

"You're acting paranoid."

"I AM paranoid!"

"I'm hiding this."

Then she runs out of the room with your phone. You try to follow her but as soon as you get out of bed you feel light-headed. You brace yourself against the bed and a dull ache in your giant ballsack becomes a radiating pain up through your left side. You feel queasy. You take two deep breaths to keep from puking, and Liesl returns.

"I powered it down. So don't try calling it."

"You don't understand these people," you say, clutching your left side. You suddenly realize you're drooling from the left side of your mouth, but you continue. "They're insane!"

*

You wake up at ten o'clock in the morning, feeling much better. The doc wasn't kidding. There's still a dull pain in your groin, and you're walking a little stiff, but besides that you feel pretty normal. You skip the painkillers and go for the ibuprofen. No shower for two days, so it's downstairs for coffee. Liesl is sitting at the kitchen table looking at her laptop.

"How are you feeling?" Liesl asks.

"Actually, pretty good," you say, and then you realize you can't really remember much from the previous day. It's a strange sensation. You remember lying in the hospital bed, talking to Liesl, but after that, it's a black hole.

"Josh Lucas," she says.

"What?"

"He's the guy from *Sweet Home Alabama*."

"What?"

She fills you in on the events of the previous day, and then it comes flooding back.

"Shit," you say. "Where's my phone?"

You have 157 emails.

Then there's another urgent email from Alice Cavanaugh-Williams, time-stamped at 8:30 this morning, which simply says, "Executive Committee Meeting today at 11:30." Although the email has been sent to you, the body of the message makes it quite clear that you are not to attend. The agenda is one item: "Status of Current Executive Director."

"You want some pancakes?" Liesl asks.

"Do you think they're bowel-friendly?"

THE VENUE

On Monday you return to work. You assume there was a meeting but no one has informed you of your status as Executive Director of Quill & Pad. Maybe they've fired you. But until somebody informs you differently, you have to fill a million dollar hole. Thankfully, the 47th most powerful man in Washington has offered his home for a fundraiser, and his nurse/receptionist Cindy has contacted you to talk about the details.

"Mr. Albert asked me to call you about a fundraiser?" she asks. "Uh, I'm...look, I'm embarrassed to ask this, I just got a post-it note to call you about the details."

"The details?"

"Yes, do you know anything about the event?" she asks.

"He offered his home for it."

"He did? Did he say what day?"

"No."

"Did he give you any idea about the format of the event, or the guests?"

"No."

She sighs, and you hear her typing.

"Let me get back to you," she says.

Exactly forty-five minutes later, Cindy calls you back.

"All right, I've got the fourteenth of December reserved; we'll be doing cocktails and dinner after some remarks by the Chief Justice."

"Of the Supreme Court?" you ask stupidly.

"Do you have some time this afternoon to come see the house?"

*

Algernon Albert's home is a modern grey fortress high in the Palisades near Georgetown. You feel like you've seen it somewhere before, but you can't place it—maybe in a magazine, or on TV, or in a movie. It sits atop a hill surrounded by tall trees in their late fall glory. You pull into the driveway, where you see Cindy waiting for you next to a Lincoln Town Car.

"Hi John," she says warmly, offering her hand. You shake it. "Thanks for making it on such short notice."

"Absolutely," you say. "Thank you for arranging all of this."

"No trouble," she smiles. "Come on in."

Cindy has keys to Albert's home, and as you enter the foyer she types in a code on a security panel, almost without looking. The foyer is enormous, with cathedral ceilings, from which are suspended huge modern tapestries, each one a different combination of colors and lines, mostly blues and greens. From the outside, the home struck you as cold and windowless, but the entire rear of the home seems to be made out of one enormous glass wall, half the length of a football field and at least twenty feet tall. It lets in an abundance of warm autumn-afternoon light, which splashes against white marble floors. The place looks like a museum, not a home, and the interior walls are covered with art. You don't know anything about art. It's not the kind of art where you know what it is.

"Mr. Albert has one of the most impressive collections of Modern Art in the world," Cindy says, as she notices you staring at a smaller, abstract piece. You notice the signature on the painting.

"Is this a Picasso?" you ask, incredulously.

"Yes. He has four."

"He has four Picassos?"

"Yes. I thought we'd do cocktails here, in the Grand Room, and then adjourn for dinner down here."

You follow her through the Albert Collection, down a small flight of stairs to a suite of rooms in a strange sub-level. This part of the home feels like a hotel. There's a meeting room, a small theater, and finally, through two massive wooden doors, you see the dining room.

The room itself is very nice, although it's functional and far less opulent than the Grand Room. It has the feeling of a country dining room, with wooden floors and a large wooden table, around which are arranged twenty tall-backed chairs. In the rear of the room there are swinging double-doors that lead to the kitchen area.

"How is this?"

"I…it's very nice. I just—how many people will we have for dinner?" you ask.

"Well, of course you and your wife have to come. That's two. Then there's Mr. and Mrs. Albert, the Chief Justice…so fifteen?"

"Fifteen guests?"

"Yes."

You nod.

"We'll invite the board, of course, but probably Alice will be the only one attending."

"What are we uh...how much..."

"Mr. Albert suggested thirty-thousand dollars a plate."

You nod, as if this amount does not shock you. You attempt to do the math in your head, arriving at $450,000.

"You think we can fill it?"

She smiles.

"I think there will be a waiting list," she says. "Mr. Albert rarely entertains. Would you like to see the library?"

*

Algernon Albert's library is located on the second floor of the house, and it's everything you've always wanted in a home. The room is roughly two-hundred square feet, and there are bookshelves everywhere, with the ladder and the little reading table, the whole shebang. Lining the wood-paneled walls there are framed, handwritten letters. Some are illegible, but the others you recognize. Ernest Hemingway. William Faulkner. T.S. Eliot. Flannery O'Connor. Tennessee Williams. The letters are addressed to various people. Editors, friends, even other writers and artists.

Cindy checks her watch. "Listen, I have to check with the staff about something. Are you all right here for a minute?"

"Absolutely," you say, running your hand over a globe. Cindy leaves the room and you wander about the library, exploring the shelves, a collection of unbelievable first editions and ancient books. In one corner, there's a bookstand holding what you think is a dictionary, but as you get closer, you see it's a First Folio.

You have only seen such a thing one other time in your life, when you were an exchange student at Oxford almost twenty years ago. That book was housed in the British Museum, behind a bulletproof glass box, and you were unable to touch it. You feel profane touching this one, running your greasy, destructive fingers down the coarse and weathered page, but you can't resist.

At one time in your life, you loved books.

"This figure, that thou here seest put, it was for gentle Shakespeare cut," quotes a woman from behind you. You turn around to see a young, impeccably dressed woman, in her mid-thirties, wearing a grey dress. She looks like she's just been steamed and pressed, her bobbed hair tight at her chin. She speaks in a thick, Eastern European accent, and you realize you've seen her before, in the painting in Algernon Albert's office. You imagined she was Albert's daughter, but that doesn't make sense, given her accent. "You have found the Folio."

"Yes. I'm sorry."

"Don't be sorry, no, no," she smiles, walking across the floor, her heels click clacking on the wood, echoing about the cavernous room. "It is to enjoy."

"I'm uh, I'm John MacManus," you say. "Quill & Pad."

"Yes, he tell me you may come by to see the house," she smiles. She's not beautiful in a conventional sense—she's odd looking, with sharp features, an aquiline nose, and huge cheekbones. She looks steely and cold, and yet she has a vampiric charm, especially with the accent.

"I am Yifgania," she says, and you take a moment to process the name.

"Nice to meet you."

"You are a Shakespeare fan?"

"Uh, yes, well," you say, turning to the Folio. "In college. I, uh, I studied—is this real?"

"Yes," she smiles.

"I just, uh, I've never seen one this close...isn't the air bad for it?"

She shrugs, stands beside you and leafs through the Folio.

You watch in agony as her long, red fingernails touch the pages, threatening to pierce them. But she doesn't.

"There is a theory now that it is better for a book to be touched. To be in the air, with a little moisture. That oil from fingers is good for pages; otherwise they dry out, become brittle. Do you have a favorite?"

"Favorite...oh, yes. *Hamlet*."

"*Hamlet*," she smiles, as if you've said something cute and stupid. "Do you know *Richard II*?"

You are embarrassed that you do not know *Richard II*. You have no idea what it's about.

"I'm sorry, I don't know it," you say.

"'Man with nothing shall be pleased, 'til he be eased with being nothing,'" she recites, closing the Folio.

Cindy re-emerges, startled by Yifgania's presence.

"Oh. Mrs. Albert," she says, and you realize that this woman is Algernon's wife. "I'm sorry, I wasn't told to expect you."

"I wanted to meet John," she says, smiling at you. "Algy speaks quite highly of you."

This news is a bit shaming to you, as you have tried to orchestrate legal maneuvers to remove Algernon from the board.

"Well, we're lucky to have him on the board."

"Yes," she says, patting you on the shoulder, somewhat menacingly. "You are."

TRIGGER

At 11:07 p.m. you are to administer your wife's Trigger Shot. You have practiced this maneuver once in the safety of a doctor's office, on a throw pillow. You have never stuck a three-inch needle into someone's ass before.

You have seen your wife's behind on a number of occasions, and you have admired it since the moment you met her. Right now, as she lies on the bed, her pants down around her ankles, there is nothing sexual about her, and you are terrified at what you are about to do. What if you hit a nerve and paralyze her or something? What if you screw up somehow? This is not an unthinkable outcome.

For the last several weeks, your wife's reproductive cycle has been strictly controlled, suppressed, and then stimulated. Now it's time to light it up! Once you administer the Trigger Shot, your wife will begin ovulating. Once this occurs, you have 24-36 hours for retrieval.

Every morning your wife has been injecting something into her abdomen that has altered her estrogen levels. You can't remember if she has more or less. You remember the statistic: "It can be as much as fifty times normal," but you don't know below or above. You've paid shockingly little attention to what your wife has been doing these past few weeks. She's seemed fine. You wouldn't know she's been injecting things at all, except that she's nauseous all the time, and there's a giant red plastic BIOHAZARD! box resting on the back of your toilet, next to the Kleenex dispenser. It's full of spent needles. Where will it go? Who will dispose of it? How?

You do know that the injections she's been administering to herself have been tinker toys compared to this bad boy, this giant fucking needle you hold in your hand, filled with your one-shot-dose of your crucial-timing Trigger Shot. The shot must be administered within a precise window of time or this cycle is a bust. That's a big problem, because then you have to skip a cycle and start over. Liesl doesn't want to start over. She doesn't want to administer shots to herself at 5:30 in the morning for another six weeks. She wants to get this over with. You would also like to get it over with.

"Well, come on, then," she says. "Let's get this show on the road!"

Once you administer this shot, something incredible will happen. The eggs will be released, and they will then be retrieved and inseminated with your frozen sperm produced with the benefit of Mexican porn, which they will "wash" and extract, selecting only the finest specimen your meager balls can produce.

The embryos will grow or not grow in isolation, and then, once they have reached a certain state of viability, they will be placed inside your wife's womb, and everything will proceed as normal. Or else it won't.

A baby will grow inside your wife. Someday, that baby will come out. When it comes out, it will require documents, nutrients, clothes, bedding, college education, automobiles, laptops, braces, toys, milk, and gasoline. You will have to shelter it, shoe it, teach it manners and character. One day it will speak back to you. One day it will ask you what you do, where it came from, what it's doing here.

One day you will have to explain yourself.

"Hurry up," Liesl says.

You kneel down on the bed next to her, holding the needle in your right hand. You practice flicking it once. The doctors have prepared you. They've taken a black magic marker and drawn a giant black "X" on your wife's ass-cheek. Everyone's been so helpful. You can't miss it. You flick it down and it penetrates your wife's skin so easily. The entire needle goes in and you push down on the plunger, like you've been doing it your whole life. Halfway through there's resistance. It's like making coffee in a French Press.

"Did you do it?" Liesl says, looking back at you. "I didn't feel anything."

*

"You have great follicles," Dr. Greenspan says creepily, staring at an ultrasound of your wife's reproductive organs.

"Really?" Liesl says hopefully. Liesl has done her homework on all this. You have little idea what's going on, but this is apparently a good sign.

"These are very nice," Dr. Greenspan says, rubbing the little thingy on your wife's stomach.

"Why do you need the gel?" you ask stupidly, referring to the green goop Dr. Greenspan unceremoniously squirted on your wife's stomach.

Liesl squeezes your hand to tell you to shut up.

"All right, I'm going to go ahead and give you the anesthesia," the doctor says, as if he's about to open presents. The nurse presses a button and the table leans back with an electronic whir. Liesl squeezes your hand again, and you feel compelled to say something.

"I'm right here," you say.

She looks at you and laughs, and then you laugh, too.

"We'll know how many eggs have proceeded to embryo tomorrow."

"And then?" Liesl asks.

"Three to five days we'll do the transfer. Until then, you need to just take it easy and relax. Go about your lives and try not to think about it. Are you ready?"

FUNDRAISER

The Chief Justice of the Supreme Court is much taller than you could have possibly imagined. He's an enormous human being, actually, with broad shoulders and mammoth hands, which he uses to great effect when relating one of his many hilarious anecdotes about life on the Supreme Court. The man's sheer size makes you consider that the rest of the Supreme Court must also be quite large, because they don't look like ants when they're sitting beside him. Then you realize that perhaps you have been living as an unthinking, subhuman servant species, so ignorant that it does not understand there is clearly a more-evolved breed out there running things. This man is fucking charming, and his wife is fucking charming, too. Elegant, beautiful, and charming. She tilts an empty wine glass by its stem, rolling her eyes as the Chief Justice talks about bow hunting with the President of the United States. He tells jokes about people you've never heard of, and the twenty people around the table are rolling in the aisles.

Then the Chief Justice sighs and taps his huge knuckles on the white tablecloth.

"But that was a long time ago. Things have gotten so nasty

in this town. Remember when Washington was a different place? Probably everyone around the table remembers. Everybody said the same nasty, crazy things, but at 5:00 p.m., they all went out for steaks and beers. And if you got somebody really good, the other guy would slap you on the back and laugh about it. There was more *sport* then. You felt it. It was competition, not war. Your kids went to the same schools, you ate in the same restaurants, you went to church together. Now? Now people can't wait to get out of this city, back to their district. Nobody *lives* here anymore. We all thought that would make it better, if everyone spent more time in their districts, right? Listening to people who really have no idea what's going on. How can they? I pity anyone who actually knows what's going on."

"That's why he's feeling so sorry for himself," his wife says to laughter. "Wrap it up, Jack."

The Chief Justice of the Supreme Court smiles, then nods as if his wife is right, placing his mammoth hand on her delicate shoulder, and somehow doing it in a thankful, non-threatening way.

"Well. All I mean to say is that it's important we occasionally get together for dinner. Get out of the echo chamber, get away from the handlers, and just sit down and speak to each other like civilized human beings. Which is why I'm so grateful to Algernon and Yifgania for inviting us into their lovely home this evening."

He raises his wine glass, and everyone raises theirs.

"And in all humility, it seems appropriate to honor our guests with a literary quote. And if I might be so arrogant as to paraphrase Montaigne…'I have never seen a greater miracle in the world…than myself.'"

Everyone laughs, toasts, and drinks, and the Chief Justice sits down. His wife rubs him on the shoulder affectionately, to let him know he did a great job. You and your wife sit at the other end of the table, trying not to stare slack-jawed at one of the most powerful couples in the world as the waiters bring you your salads. "To paraphrase Montaigne." You don't know who the fuck Montaigne is, and you're the guy who's supposed to know. You think he lived during the Renaissance. You imagine that the Chief Justice of the Supreme Court knows Montaigne's life story, has visited his childhood home, and is likely able to summon up entire tomes of quotations from Montaigne's obscure correspondence. He's that guy.

Quill & Pad is never mentioned. You doubt that the people at this dinner know or care what they're giving money to. They're giving money to sit at the table with one another. By the time they serve you a ridiculously rare piece of meat, Algernon Albert is asleep and snoring, but his thirty-year-old wife is engaged in conversation with a sandy-haired gentleman in a brown sport coat. You don't know his name, but he's an attorney. You don't know anybody's names, but they're all attorneys—everyone except Alice Cavanaugh-Williams, who sits opposite Albert with a young man who must be her son. The young man is a Marine, and he's dressed in formal Marine garb. He has a fucking sword.

As for the others, who are they? They're people who can afford to drop $30,000 on a week's notice to have dinner on a random Tuesday.

"This is the craziest dinner I've ever been to," Liesl whispers to you, and you smile. You're so grateful she's here. Liesl can talk to anyone, and does, as she makes conversation with the woman sitting next to you. The woman next to you is also an attorney. She's maybe forty-five, and she wears a grey pantsuit that is clearly ten or fifteen years out of style.

"But I haven't practiced in years," she says, carving up her steak and putting a thick piece in her mouth. She talks with her mouth full, waving her fork around. "I went to school with Vivian Albert."

"Is that…" Liesl asks.

"His first wife. Two wives ago. Well. Was. You know. Before she hung herself," she says casually, popping another piece of meat in her mouth. It's loud enough at the table that no one else can hear her.

"Oh my god, how awful," Liesl says.

"You don't know this story?" the woman asks, nodding to the snoring Algernon with her fork. "Algernon was the one who found her. Up in their house on the Vineyard. I guess she'd been there a couple weeks."

You suddenly dislike this woman very much, as she routinely relates the grisly details of Algernon Albert discovering his wife's rotting corpse hanging from a rafter of his summer home.

"You can see how it could happen. He was different back then. Very hard-charging. They basically lived apart. Also how would anybody know for a couple weeks? Especially in October. After Labor Day, everyone disappears. Algernon won't go back up there anymore. But he can't let go of the house, so Yifgania's up there occasionally in the summer. Just to keep up appearances, I think. That all happened a long time before Yifgania. He married Julie after that. Or Mary, maybe? Oh, have you met Mary? We play bridge together now. Which is kind of funny. I mean she's younger than I am. I used to babysit her."

"When was this?" you ask.

"Oh, way back, a long time ago. I guess—God—twenty years? Twenty-five, maybe?"

You look over to the 47th most powerful man in Washington, who's enjoying a nice nap, and you hope nobody wakes him up.

*

After dinner you have cocktails in the gallery, where Alice

Cavanaugh-Williams is delighted to meet your lovely wife.

"Are you Liesl?" she asks coquettishly. "You are the loveliest thing I've ever seen. I *adore* that bag."

"Thank you," Liesl says. Liesl is aware that this woman has tried to fire you on numerous occasions. Her handbag is a Coach knockoff she purchased at TJ Maxx. "It's a pleasure to meet you. John's told me a lot about you."

"Well, we just think the *world* of John at Quill & Pad," she says, smiling, and then she introduces you both to the six-foot-four Marine standing next to her. "This is my son, Beechum."

"Nice to meet you," you say, offering your hand. He's wearing white gloves. He shakes your hand like he's going to break it in half, but he's got a very pleasant smile and he's quite an affable young man. He asks you how you're working with his mom.

"You must have a lot of patience. She can be a bit of a challenge," he smiles.

"Oh, Beechum," she says, slapping his shoulder. Beechum doesn't do a lot of talking. You have never met a Beechum before. It's an old family name. Beechum is a Captain in the United States Marine Corps. Beechum enlisted after 9/11. Beechum has served two tours in Iraq, for which he has received all sorts of medals, commendations, and awards, displayed prominently in ribbons and little colored bars on his blue dress uniform. The only one you understand is the Purple Heart. Beechum has killed people with his bare hands. Beechum was wounded saving two men in his company in an ambush near Fallujah.

"Really, it was nothing," he says. "I got grazed on my right arm and they made a big deal out of it."

"He's just being modest," Alice says.

"No, I'm telling the truth," he says, somewhat annoyed. "There are guys—there are *men* who have been wounded a lot worse than I have, doing a lot more, and nobody made such a big deal about it. I guess that's just because of who I am. I did what any of those men would do, and have done."

You have never seen a man stand straighter than Beechum Cavanaugh-Williams. If he were standing any straighter he'd be bending backwards.

"Well. Thank you for your service," you say stupidly, because you don't know what else to say. You are awed by Beechum Cavanuagh-Williams, the Fortunate Son who certainly did not need to join the military, let alone the goddamned Marines. He's a handsome, modest, billionaire war hero, and you wonder how a woman like Alice Cavanuagh-Williams could've possibly raised a man like this.

*

At 10:00 the evening is over. The Chief Justice and his wife shake your wife's hand, and then they shake your hand and tell you what a pleasure it was to meet you. Yifgania hands you an envelope full of checks.

"I'm sorry Algernon didn't make it," she says. "He has a hard time staying up late."

"Of course, thank you," you say, accepting the envelope awkwardly. "Will you thank him for me?"

"Of course," she says, turning to Liesl. "Liesl. Such a pleasure. I hope you'll be my guest on the Vineyard this summer."

"Uh..." Liesl stammers. "Thank you, I've never been."

"Well. The only thing is, you have to learn to play bridge," Yifgania says, rolling her eyes. "I'll teach you."

"Thank you," Liesl says. "Thank you for everything."

"Of course," she says, nodding at the envelope in your hand. "Don't worry about the thank yous. I'll take care of them."

"I don't know what to say," you say.

"Be nice to him." Yifgania says, holding up her finger. "Please don't kick him off the board."

"Uh. Right. No. Of course," you stammer, surprised and ashamed.

*

They have people who bring your car around, and you debrief about the evening. What people wore, why didn't we get a picture with the Chief Justice, can you believe that woman next to you, and what is wrong with Alice Cavanaugh-Williams?

"I totally see what you mean," Liesl says. "What a condescending bitch, talking about my bag like that. And who names their kid Beechum?"

"I know."

"Beechum was kind of awesome though. No offense. He's kinda hot."

"None taken. I wanted to go home with him."

"I bet you did. Seriously, that guy's gonna be President someday."

"I'd vote for him."

"It's awful about that guy's wife. Algernon. Did you know that?"

"No."

"I don't think he knew people were actually there. Poor guy. And can you believe Yifgania inviting me to the Vineyard? Oh my god, what if I'm pregnant then?"

"That'd be great. You, me, Algernon, and his twenty-year-old vampire wife, playing Uno on the Vineyard."

She laughs.

"Tonight was pretty fun," she says.

"Yeah," you say. "It's a nice place to visit. They know how to entertain."

"That house is amazing."

"Yeah," and then you pause. "It's easy to forget you're not one of them."

"I know," she says quietly, looking out the window. "But still."

"But you had fun, though, right?"

"Oh my god, it was great," she says. "Surreal. How much money did you make?"

"Four-hundred-and-fifty-thousand," you say, patting your lapel.

"Holy shit! You have half-a-million bucks in your pocket," she says. "Better keep your eye on the road."

And you do, for as a seasoned Washingtonian you now use the Rock Creek Parkway, a road that requires you pay attention. And on the dark corners of Rock Creek Parkway, you wonder how far $450,000 would take you, if you could cash all those checks and leave town today. How long would you last on $450,000? You do the math in your head as you cross the bridge to Virginia, as your wife nods off next to you.

There's your underwater mortgage back in Chicago at $250,000. A car loan at $12,000. Student loans north of $58,000. And don't forget Shared Promise at $25,000.

And as you subtract these amounts in your head, rather poorly, in a ridiculous exercise that assumes you stole half-a-million dollars and then dutifully paid all your debts, you realize that you might walk away in the end with a hundred grand. That might last a year, maybe two years if you were frugal. It's nowhere near enough to raise a child. Without health insurance, you'd probably spend most of it just delivering the baby.

Driving south on Route 1 you're just approaching the

Pentagon when you wonder: *Jesus. Wasn't there a time when half-a-million dollars was a lot of fucking money?*

TRANSFER

The doctors have given you a picture of your blastocyst. The blastocyst is a group of cells that will eventually grow into your child.

"We have a very small camera," the nurse says, making air quotes around "small camera." Then she winks at you.

The blastocyst appears to you like something you might see in a kaleidoscope. It is a symmetrical, metallic green group of circles. They give it to you on something like a Polaroid, tucked into a little card with a pocket, as a memento of your conception journey. The card has Shared Promise's logo on it, and inside the word "Congratulations!" is written in cursive, in sparkly silver ink. Perhaps you should send it out as a Christmas card.

"Thank you," you say, staring at the picture.

"Can I see it?" Liesl asks, lying on a table, her feet suspended in stirrups.

You hand her the picture and she looks at it. You think it's decidedly old school that she's lying there with her feet up in the air. After the hormone injections, Trigger Shot, sperm-washing, and genetic manipulation, maybe in the end gravity will help that little blastocyst attach.

"Can't hurt!" the doctor says before exiting the room with great speed.

Your phone dings. You have an email. Your phone dings whenever you get emails. You've tried turning it off but it doesn't work. Somehow it resets every time you recharge your phone or plug it into your computer.

"You can check it," Liesl says.

"It's okay."

"Why not," she says, handing you the Christmas card. "We're just waiting. Actually, can you get mine?"

You wonder how they did it 1,000 years ago. Did witches come and sit in your yurt, gossiping with one another, pouring calf's blood around a hearth for desperate couples? Oh, how their lives would've been improved by Angry Birds and Facebook Scrabble.

You have received an email from Alice Cavanaugh-Williams's assistant, who has summoned you to a meeting with the Grand Dame sometime around 6:30 this evening. On a Friday. On the day when you and your wife are hoping to conceive a child.

"Why don't they just fire you?" Liesl asks.

"I don't know," you sigh. "I wish they would."

"We need to think positive thoughts."

Yes. But you also need to pay a $4,000 deposit.

*

You find yourself in the white room again, staring at the same decorative books, and this time there are no radishes and hummus. The servants are very busy, arranging the house for some kind of fête. It's a great house for entertaining. Perhaps they'll use the fireplace in the backyard.

It's only 7:00 p.m. and it's already dark outside. People are working around you like you're not there. Two workmen set up a podium in the front of the room, near the bay window overlooking the turnaround, and then a twenty-something kid steps up to the lectern. He does not acknowledge you. The room is fairly large, and you're on opposite ends of it, so it's understandable. He's wearing a blue blazer and khaki pants. He looks like somebody just dressed him up for Winter Formal. He adjusts the podium mic and taps it, and you hear the sound in the back of the room.

"Test test," he says, and he unfolds a piece of paper and clears his throat. "Brian, can you check the levels?" he asks, and a man in black pants and a turtleneck walks in the room. This is Brian. Brian looks like a roadie. He's got a huge grey beard and he looks like a crumpled-up pack of cigarettes. He's wearing a set of headphones, and he twirls his finger to signal the kid to start speaking.

"All right? Okay?" the kid asks, and then reads. "The governor's position on education can be summed up in one word: accountability. We want to make sure that tax dollars are being spent efficiently in schools that work, for teachers that work for those dollars. There are no excuses for poor performance. Look, our public schools are failing, especially in urban areas like right here in the district. It's not a question of resources. We're pumping resources into these schools, but test scores are not improving. In some instances, we're actually seeing a decline in results, especially in critical areas like math and science. China and India are outperforming American students, and you know why? They don't accept excuses. We can't be shackled by the soft bigotry of low expectations. How's that? How's that Brian?"

Brian rolls his finger in the air to signal for him to keep reading.

"Uh...okay, so...all right...India, China...soft bigotry...here.

The problem is that teachers are not being held accountable for the performance of their students. In any other line of work, if you got results like these, you'd be fired. But the teachers' unions make excuse after excuse for failing teachers. The governor's success in the private sector is a result of accepting no excuses. It's time to hold teachers accountable, like everyone else who earns a paycheck in this struggling economy....Got it?"

"We're good to go," Brian says, stepping out of the doorway.

The kid steps away from the podium and nods at you. You don't know what to do, so you nod back.

"Mr. MacManus?" the old butler says. "Mrs. Cavanaugh-Williams will be with you in a moment."

SIX MONTHS LATER

LOGISTICS

Every other Friday for the last six months you have been summoned unceremoniously to Alice Cavanaugh-Williams's home. The actual purpose of these summons is unknown to you, as you generally wait for about an hour before you are told that Mrs. Cavanaugh-Williams has a scheduling conflict and apologizes deeply. You assume the real reason behind all this is simply to make your life unpleasant. And it does make your life unpleasant, especially as your wife is now six months pregnant, and tends to fall asleep at 7:30 on Friday evenings, after an exhausting week on her feet in front of classrooms full of apathetic children.

The Quill & Pad benefit is now only four weeks away. For the first time in the dim memory of the organization, the benefit has sold out. This would be good news, except for the fact that even with $1 million in revenue, you are set to spend $1.2 million to produce the event, meaning your fundraiser is $200,000 in the red. In fact, if it weren't for this $200,000 shortfall, you would almost have a balanced budget. So what you have on your hands is a huge success that looks an awful lot like failure, and which will *really* look like a failure about a month after the benefit, when the

175

fiscal year comes to a close. When that happens, a giant house of cards will come crashing down upon your head.

Your baby is due a month after this disaster occurs, and you have not prepared the home. You have read *What to Expect When You're Expecting.* You have acquired various strange gifts and contraptions that require assembly. A swing. A crib. A bassinet. A changing table. All in boxes, crammed into a deathtrap of a room filled with electrical sockets, bookcases, sharp corners, and god knows what else. You've been cramming baby materials into the guest room, waiting for a weekend to sort it all out. And meanwhile there have been ultrasounds and progress reports. It will be a girl. All her chromosomes appear to be in the right place. You have seen her little heart beating, the twinkle in Liesl's womb, her little face, and even on one scan, what appeared to be your child sucking her thumb.

You will require life insurance and long-term disability. You will need to establish a college fund. You need to get a car seat and have it inspected. You need to get a new job, and you have tried to get a new job. You have sent out hundreds of resumes; you have contracted with a headhunter; you have filled out dozens of online forms asking about your work habits, your three biggest weaknesses, your ability to work in fast-paced team environments.

So far you have had one interview, with a policy association in DuPont. The former Executive had been forced out by his board, and yet they weirdly retained him to oversee the transition. The Executive took full advantage of this by signing an exorbitant, ten-year lease in DuPont and hiring a strange transvestite to manage their computer servers. You went to this interview. You met Sandy. The cross-dressing didn't bother you. Sandy's discussion of her bipolar disorder bothered you, as she blamed her condition alternately on her stint in the infantry and her cats. She'd apparently acquired a common parasite transmitted through their feces.

"It gets in your brain, you know," she said. "It's scientific."

"Isn't she great?" the Executive said, grinning ear to ear. "Of course, we have to accommodate Sandy's schedule with a generous flex time. Sandy manages The Cloud."

Sadly, an offer of employment was not forthcoming.

And so soon you will be unemployed, disgraced, and without any prospects. You will be supported by your wife, a high school English teacher, as you change diapers and clip coupons and explain to your infant daughter: *Daddy drove a company to bankruptcy. Daddy killed an American literary institution. Yes he did! Goo goo ga ga!*

"Mrs. Cavanaugh-Williams will see you now," the servant tells you. What an unexpected treat. You follow the servant through a labyrinth of strange and purposeless rooms. There is a room with a desk and a harpsichord, a small room with a plush leather chair and a reading lamp, and a long, parlor-type room with red chaise lounges that could potentially be arranged for a reasonably festive Roman orgy.

Finally you reach a small white door, and behind it you find Alice Cavanaugh-Williams sitting at a tiny, bird-like desk covered in papers. The desk looks like it belongs in a dollhouse. It has tiny, spindly legs and matching tiny chairs, one of which is occupied by Kathy Apple, your event planner. Behind the desk, Alice sits with small reading spectacles attached by a chain around her head, examining papers. She flips through them. She does not greet you. Kathy Apple does not greet you. You sit in the unoccupied chair and wait for someone to address you. After a few minutes of awkward silence, Alice breaks the silence.

"I don't want shrimp. Everybody will eat shrimp and nobody will bother with the dinner."

"I agree completely," Kathy says.

You nod but say nothing. Alice flaps another page down on the desk. She holds a picture at arm's length and sighs.

"I don't like these table dressings," she says, holding a picture of a place setting away from her face. "It's too elaborate. I want it elegant and simple."

"I don't know why they even sent you that one," Kathy says. "I told them not to."

"I don't want them to look cheap," Alice says. "When is the dessert tasting?"

"Thursday.'"

"Thursday," she says, flipping a date book open. "What time on Thursday?"

"10:00 a.m."

"10:00 a.m. for a tasting?" Alice asks. "You'll need to be there, John."

"All right," you say.

"Well, are you free?" Alice asks.

"Of course."

"Desserts make or break events," Alice says quickly, scribbling down a note in her datebook. "People remember desserts. What's going on with the speaker?"

"We're all set," you assure her.

"Has he been contracted?"

"Yes."

"Travel's arranged?"

"Of course."

"I like to give out copies of the book as party favors," she says, scribbling something down. "Have you ordered the books?"

"We have the books. In my office."

Alice stares up.

"Excuse me? You have six-hundred books in your office?"

"Yes."

"Well, that must be very crowded," Alice says, in a rare moment of sympathy.

"I'd like to bring up the calligrapher again," Kathy says. "Alice, we really need to use the calligrapher for the place cards. I know you're trying to cut corners but this is a matter of basic..."

"We can print the placecards," Alice says, checking something off in her book.

"But it's a matter of *appearances*, and with all due respect, I don't think you're really..."

Alice glares at her.

"We're printing the placecards, Kathy. I'm not spending five-thousand dollars for a few hundred placecards."

"People keep these; they take them home..."

"Excuse me, Kathy, but I go to one of these goddamned things every week. Sometimes twice a week," Alice says sharply, pointing her pen at Kathy. "And I have never, ever—not once—kept a place card as a souvenir."

"Well, I'm not..."

"It's ridiculous. What you're saying is ridiculous."

"Quill & Pad has had hand-written placecards for three decades, and I think don't you understand the value of tradition..."

"I'm happy to take it out of your fee if you think they're so essential," Alice says. This exchange surprises you, and you watch Kathy Apple fold her legs and lean back in her ignominious placecard smackdown.

"I just think you run the risk of looking cheap."

Alice shoots her a look. It's tense for a moment, but then Alice smiles and rummages through the mountain of papers on her desk for something.

"John. I understand you're expecting," she says.

"Yes,"

"And your wife? How is she doing? I'm sorry I don't recall

her name."

"Liesl," you say. "It's Liesl. She's doing well."

"How far along is she?"

"Six months."

"Six months," she smiles, finding a small envelope, which she hands to you. Your name is handwritten on the front. As she hands it to you, you notice Kathy Apple squirm nervously in her seat. "This is your first, am I right?"

"Yes," you say.

"Some people never know the joy of being a parent," she says, nodding to Kathy.

"Yes ma'am."

"Boy or girl? Or do you know?"

"It's a girl."

"A girl," she smiles. "All I ever had were boys, boys, boys. How lovely. A little baby girl. Have you thought about names?"

"Yes, but, we're...we're a little superstitious about it."

"Of course, of course, I'm sorry to pry," she says. "And have you thought about what you're going to do when the baby comes?"

"Uh..."

"I mean as far as Quill & Pad is concerned. Have you thought about taking some time off?"

"Yes," you say, resisting the urge to tell her that you expect a permanent vacation about a month afterwards.

"You'll need lots of help," Alice says, leaning back in her chair. "Is your mother coming?"

"Well, yes, after Liesl's parents."

"Good. Good. It's all a blur, that time. That first year or two after they arrive. Beechum, he was a colicky baby. Fussy all the time. Would barely eat. Slept an hour at a time. And you'll be amazed how they come out. Everybody's always...everybody's always so generous about Beechum. They think we had something to do with it, David and I. But they come out how they come out, and all the raising in the world won't change them an inch."

You nod.

"We'll try not to do these on Friday nights anymore," she says. "I'm sorry to have kept you so late. Your wife must be very cross with us."

"Not at all," you shrug.

She looks back down at her datebook and begins writing.

"Well. We'll see you at the tasting then. Don't be late."

*

Liesl is asleep when you get home. For the last few weeks, she's been falling asleep at seven or eight. It started on the couch, as she tried to pretend to be watching television, but now she's given up the ghost and heads up to bed after dinner.

You take off your coat and crack open a beer. You've almost forgotten about the envelope in your suit pocket. You're expecting a bill, or perhaps a donation for the benefit.

It's a personal check made out to you in the amount of ten-thousand dollars.

CHECKUP

"So she just gave you $10,000?" Liesl says, sitting on the gynecologist's table. You realize as she's sitting there that she looks much more pregnant than she did just a few weeks ago. Liesl's been having pains. You receive emails from some strange website that explains everything before it happens. The strange pains are perfectly normal. At six months, your baby is forming sweat glands. The baby is over a foot long now. Liesl's feet look nearly twice their normal size. That is called edema. Edema is perfectly normal. There are things you should be doing. You should be making a birth plan. You should be painting the nursery now. You should assemble the crib, start a college fund, settle on a name. You are behind on everything.

"Yep."

"I thought she wanted to fire you."

"She does want to fire me."

"It doesn't sound like it."

"I'm actually more worried about it now that she gave me the money."

"Why?"

"I think she did it to make a point or something."

"About what?"

"Not to me, to Kathy Apple."

"Why would giving you ten-thousand dollars make a point to Kathy Apple?"

"You can't try to understand what motivates these people," you caution. "They're insane."

"Well. It's good to have anyway. I wish someone would give me $10,000," Liesl says. "Get this—they want me to do yearbook now."

"You're six months pregnant."

"No shit. Bob's been all over my ass about how great I am at layout. It's ten hours a week, two whole Saturdays on top of that, and guess how much they want to pay me? Guess?"

"I don't know. Five grand?"

"Ha! Five grand! How about zero grand? Two-hundred dollars. That's what they want to pay me. Two-hundred dollars. That's before taxes."

"Well, you're not doing it, right?"

"No! Well. I don't know, then they make you feel terrible, like the kids won't have a yearbook unless I do it."

"Fuck the kids."

"Babe. Come on."

"No, I'm serious. You have to take it easy. You have to think about yourself."

"Yeah. I know," she says, rubbing her hand over her tummy. "This is normal, right?"

"Yeah."

"I mean, I haven't felt her move for a while. That's normal."

"The email says they get cramped in there. She probably doesn't have a good angle."

"I'm huge."

"You're not huge. It's normal."

"I look like I'm nine months already."

"Well, she's big."

"*I'm* big. I need to eat more fruit. Do we have any frozen raspberries?"

The gynecologist comes in. She's relatively famous for having delivered the first Washingtonian of the new millennium. There was an article about it in the *Washington Post*, and a copy of it now hangs on the wall, under the heading, "Millennium Baby Arrives!" The gynecologist holds a chart and wears pink-framed glasses which are secured to her body by a long chain dropping at her shoulders.

"Hi Liesl, how are we feeling?"

"I'm okay. But I haven't felt her move in a while. Is that normal?"

"Let's take a look," the doctor says, leaning Liesl back on the table and squeezing out some ultrasound jelly on her stomach. She sits on a wheeled stool and pulls a monitor over to the bedside, and there you see your daughter, all twelve inches of her. You see a shudder on the screen.

"What is that?" you ask.

"She's got some hiccups," the doctor says, moving the ultrasound paddle down and around.

"She does?" Liesl says, straining to see.

"She looks very cozy in there."

"Oh my god, she's got the hiccups," Liesl says.

"She's fine. Everything looks fine. I'm a little concerned though about your blood pressure," the gynecologist says. "Obviously, it's going to be a little elevated, but I'm a little concerned that it really hasn't changed since two weeks ago. How are you sleeping?"

"Great," Liesl says. "I'm a little stressed out at work."

"It's not in that 'danger zone,' yet, but we're getting close—I need you to stay off your feet. Can you put your feet up at work?"

"I'm a teacher. I'm on my feet all day."

"Not anymore you're not," the doctor says, writing something on a piece of paper. "You give your principal this if they give you any trouble. You need to sit more and keep your feet elevated. That should help reduce some of the swelling too. Is it painful?"

"Only when I stand," Liesl says.

THE WEEK FROM SRI LANKA

Despite the fact that the board of Quill & Pad is now distributing random $10,000 bonuses to its employees, the organization has officially begun to run out of money. This has occurred two months before you expected it to happen, giving you further proof that you are not a genius. Technically, you still have money. But two months ago, you let the intern go because you couldn't afford the $1,000-a-month stipend. It's now down to you and one other staffer, the Deputy, and the Deputy's no dummy. She's been looking around just like you.

The only reason that the music hasn't stopped is that there's money coming in for the benefit, but as of yet, no bills. No hotel bill, no catering bill, and except for the insane $100,000 deposit, nothing more from Kathy Apple. But you're spending that money now, and you know it. Every moment of your salary, your health insurance, and your utilities are coming out of money you're going to owe other people in just three months.

A strange numbness about all this has settled in on you. You still wake up in the middle of the night, breathless and sweating. You very much understand what it means. But day-to-day, you don't seem to think about it anymore. It's coming, and there's nothing you can do to stop it. You've tried to find the money. You've tried to get fired. You've tried to find another job. But you are now down to it. And when it happens, it will be awful. More awful than you think it's going to be, and you know this. It should be right around the time that Liesl goes on maternity leave. That should be convenient. You'll both have plenty of time to spend with the new baby. No money and a lot of disgrace. But plenty of time. Plenty of time to look into starting that college fund for the baby. Plenty of time to pack your shit and move, and have your car repossessed, and go live with your parents or your in-laws. What a treat that will be. They can help with the baby. You'll be busy in depositions.

Until then, you busy yourself with the minutiae of planning a black-tie benefit for the most powerful people in Washington. It's like planning a shotgun wedding for 600 guests who despise one another. Alice and Kathy insist on handling the seating, and that's fine with you. Your work is fairly mundane—preparing tax receipts, reviewing linen samples, checking itineraries. You keep a nice running tally of bills. Half-a-million and counting.

Monday

On Monday you get a call from Sandi at the Ritz Carlton. Sandi is your Designated Event Liaison. You've met her on site visits before. She always buys you a coffee in the lobby ("My treat!"). Sandi looks like she could be a swimsuit model. She has a great smile and very nice business cards. She's very friendly. Anything she can do to help you.

"Hiiiii John," she purrs over the phone. "How you holding up?"

"Sandi, I'm dandy," you say.

"Dandy, huh? Gearing up for the big event. Right around the corner."

"Yes it is."

"Hey, I know you've got a *thousand* details to go over, but I just got a call from accounting, and…you know how these people are, they're saying they need a deposit."

"A deposit?"

"For the event. It's *reeeallly* annoying, but they're claiming that last year there were some complications. Vanessa was *reeeaallly* great to work with, but sometimes she didn't dot all the i's and cross the t's, if you know what I mean."

"Oh…" you say, quickly retrieving your hotel contract, which was signed before you came on board. The hotel contract clearly states that the hotel may request a 25% deposit in some instances, which would come to about $50,000. You do have $50,000. But if you give the hotel that money, you'll have to skip the little things this month. Like payroll, rent, taxes, and health insurance. You think about your plan. Your plan is to stiff people like the Ritz Carlton. You are not likely to get away with this plan.

"*Annnnyway*, I hate to be a *nag* about it, we've been doing Quill & Pad for years, but you know how these bean counters can be."

"Well, see—Sandi, the thing is, you know this benefit is what really drives our budget," you say quickly, coming up with some incredible bullshit. "And, I know this is bizarre, but most of the attendees pay after the event. You know. So…is there any way we could get a waiver on that deposit?"

"Oh, John, I'm sure we can figure something out," she says. "I love Quill & Pad."

Tuesday

Your Deputy resigns. She's a nice person. You haven't seen a whole lot of her the last couple weeks, but you wish her the best.

"Where are you going?"

"The National Cystic Fibrosis Society," she says. You recognize this name. It's where the previous Executive Director of Quill & Pad wound up.

"So you'll be working with Vanessa?"

"She hired me."

"Are there any openings?"

"Ha."

"Well, good luck."

"Yeah," she says, standing up, shaking your hand. "You know it's nothing personal, right?"

"Absolutely," you say. "You're doing the right thing."

"Thanks. Listen, I know this is the worst time to bring this up, but when they—when the board hired me, they gave me this agreement…"

She hands you a copy of a contract you've never seen before.

"Yeah, well—listen, I know things are—look, John, honestly, I know this is just, well, I know it's all fucked up, and it's not your fault, but technically, when they hired me, when Vanessa hired me, they gave me this bonus incentive, because I was making more money at my last job, they said they'd give me a $5,000 bonus each year, but every year they kept rolling it over, and that was okay, I understood…but now…Now? Well. It's four years. It's $20,000."

You nod. You read her contract.

"It's just…I mean that's a lot of money to me…"

You get out the checkbook and write her a check for $20,000. She looks stunned, like she didn't expect it, as if she came in thinking she would have to fight you for half of it. And momentarily, you're hurt, you're offended that she might've thought this.

"I know you don't have this," she says. "You can pay me after the benefit…"

"If you don't take it now, you're not going to get it."

"Oh," she says, looking at the check. "Well…you know, I don't…I don't need it that bad…"

"Quill & Pad made a commitment to you," you say. "If you can't keep your word, and honor your commitments, then what are you?"

This is the man you'd like to believe you are. This is who you want this poor girl to remember you as. The generous, self-sacrificing type, the man who kept his word. As you lie to vendors and cash your own check first. And in this moment, how right you feel, how noble, how satisfied.

But when she thanks you, and leaves your office, your stomach drops, and for a moment you consider stopping payment on the check.

Wednesday

The tasting is upon you! Why your presence is required at the tasting is a mystery. You are certainly not here to give your opinion. As usual, no expense has been spared. The caterer is well-known in town. She caters receptions for all the top events. The facility is located in Northeast, and it's certainly more industrial than you would've expected. It's a flat-looking warehouse surrounded by a chain link fence, atop which rests bundles of barbed wire. Inside the fence, however, there are manicured walkways and lush trees leading you to the greeting area where a receptionist in a crisp white bodysuit takes your coat and offers you espresso.

She leads you to the Tasting Area, which is a small banquet room that appears to have been decorated by an unused villain from the 1960s *Batman* television show. The room looks schizophrenic, and it's designed to show three different room set-ups. The first is black-and white elegance, with two eight-top white tables set just-so, with tasteful votive candles accenting staid floral centerpieces. The second third of the room is eclectic and colorful, with pale turquoise tablecloths and bright orange plates surrounding tall arrangements of huge Gerber daises. And the final third of the room is art-deco, with black tables covered in thin white linens with checkered edges, on top of which rest square white serving plates and thin glass decanters filled with single red roses. It smells like a florist's shop.

Alice and Kathy Apple are sitting in the elegant section, sipping wine and laughing. A woman in a white chef's outfit and a huge chef's hat greets you and shakes your hand vigorously. She's in her mid-forties, with sandy brown hair just peaking out from the edge of the chef's hat.

"Welcome, welcome," she says. "I'm Jessica,"

"Jessica is *the* best," Kathy Apple tells you, by way of warning.

"It's nice to meet you," you say.

"Come, sit," she says, seating you adjacent to Alice and Kathy, but in the eclectic section.

Immediately a man in a tuxedo appears carrying a tray of six wine glasses. Two whites, one red. He tells you all about them. You know nothing about wine, and even though you like to drink, you never acquired a taste for it.

"This Pinot is fabulous," Alice says. She seems happy. Alice has seemed happy lately. She hasn't even tried to fire you recently.

"Goes well with the veal medallions," Kathy Apple says.

"I don't know if I care for the medallions," Alice says.

"What else do we have?"

"I think you should try it with the braised bison," Chef Jessica suggests. She tells you all about the braised bison, about where it was raised, what it was fed, where it went to school, how it is sliced and prepared over roasted fingerling potatoes and a marmalade slaw. All of this sounds pretty good, and then you're brought a plate with your choices. Veal, bison, filet, duck, and trout.

"The trout. Is out," Alice laughs. She seems practically giddy. Actually, she appears to be drunk, all seventy-five pounds of her all a-titter, her giant gold necklace shaking against her silver dress as she laughs. She sets down her wine glass and motions for another. "I love tastings."

"You're right, Alice," Kathy says. "The bison is *delicious*. I've never had it prepared this way. I thought it would be tough."

"It's a terrific protein," Jessica notes. "So do we think the bison and the Pinot for service?"

"Yes. What do you think, John?" Alice asks.

"Um. Yes, it's great. Is there a uh...is there a price differential?"

Chef Jessica looks a little taken aback. She looks to Kathy, who looks appalled, and then to Alice, who gives her a little wave, as if to forget it.

"John's always trying to cut corners," she says, rolling her eyes. "It's the bison, Jessica."

"It really is tremendous," Kathy adds.

"Excellent. But to answer your question, this particular pairing, with the dessert selection and the salad—and the passed hors d'oeuvres of course—we'll be at $275 a plate."

You nod. 600 plates. $275 each. $165,000. Not including the bar. Not including the hotel.

"Can I try the Pinot again?" you ask.

Thursday

The Ritz Carlton graciously agrees to accept a $25,000 deposit. You are running out of money.

Friday

Your phone rings. It's Nadia, Hector Siffuentes' assistant. She has some exciting news for you.

"I'm afraid Hector will have to cancel," she says. Nadia's been calling with various extremely specific requests for the past several months. With less than a month before the event, you doubt you can find a replacement, and certainly not a Gay Latino Poet replacement that would satisfy Alice Cavanaugh-Williams.

"I see," you say, taking out the folder with his speaker agreement. "Can you tell me why?"

You hear the muffled noise of a man talking to Nadia on the other end of the line.

"He's feeling called to Sri Lanka."

"He's feeling called," you say, pinching the bridge of your nose.

"He's feeling called by the suffering of the people of Sri Lanka."

"I'm sorry to hear that," you say. "About the suffering."

"Of course, we'll return your honoraria."

"Of course," you say. "Nadia, do you have a copy of the speaker agreement there?"

You hear her asking Hector something. You are very tired of Hector and Nadia. You have handled difficult speakers before. It is why you have one clause inserted into every speaker agreement. That clause states that within eight weeks of the event, any cancellation for any reason will subject the speaker to assume marketing and production costs for the event. You don't know how much Gay Latino Poets make on an annual basis, but you doubt it's enough to cover Kathy Apple's fee, let alone the catering, the invitations, and a half-dozen rooms at the Ritz Carlton.

"Uh, I'm...working from home today," Nadia says.

"That's okay. I've got your email. I can email you a PDF. There. Just sent it. Did you get it?"

"Uh..."

"I'll wait."

"Got it."

"Go ahead and scroll down to page seven, section eight, where it lists the cancellation terms. Do you see that?"

"Yes."

"Okay. Well, where should I send the bill for the event? I'm happy to email you a copy. It should come to about...I think it's eight-hundred grand."

Nadia says something to Hector.

"Nadia?" you ask again. "Are you there?"

"Uh, yes, I'm here."

"So should I email you a bill, or do you need it overnighted? I'm glad to FedEx you a copy."

"I don't...we, uh..."

"Or should I send it somewhere in Sri Lanka? Will the ghost be going, too?"

"Are you trying to be rude?"

"No."

There's a silence on the other end of the line. You don't care about Nadia or Hector or Sri Lanka. And it would be great if Haunted Gay Latino Poets could be sued for enough money to rescue you from your problems. But they can't. Until that day, you're gonna squeeze Hector Siffuentes's balls until they're blue and bursting.

That's when the building starts shaking. It starts slow at first, and it's almost like a large truck is rolling right by your office, which is near the White House. But then the shaking gets more severe, and books begin falling off your shelves. The windows rattle. Oh god. Oh god, it's a terrorist attack. Oh shit, someone's slammed a plane into the White House. *Now your commute is fucked!*

But the shaking doesn't stop. It keeps going and going, until you're thrown out of your chair. You hear people screaming outside, and you stumble up to your feet. You have no idea what is occurring. All you know is not to take the elevator. You burst through the fire escape door, down the cement steps to the back alley. Is that what you're supposed to do? You're doing it. You're outside in the alley, and there are people all over the streets, looking around confused.

"It's an earthquake!" somebody yells. "EARTHQUAKE!"

And it is. An earthquake. In Washington, DC You're standing on the ground with no idea what to do. What's the protocol? All you can remember is stop drop and roll. It goes over and over again in your head. Stop drop and roll. That's not right. Tall buildings surround you, and you can see them wavering, tilting. Bits of brick and dust fly off them. Large chunks slam into the pavement. You try to find some wide-open space but there isn't any. People stagger around Pennsylvania Avenue, helpless and confused. There are sirens. You hear something loud, something like a steam whistle, and overhead five fighter jets scream across the sky, in a perfect V like a flock of geese, low enough that you could almost touch them.

"Oh god," somebody yells. "Oh god."

EARTHQUAKE!

The landlord is in your unfinished basement with a flashlight. He shines his light up at the cement walls, and you have no idea what you're looking for. You don't think he knows what he's looking for. Yesterday there was an earthquake in Washington, DC, measuring 5.8 on the Richter scale. This was the first earthquake in Washington in more than a century. Long before your townhouse was built, architects had stopped factoring in the possibility of earthquakes during construction.

"Was that crack here before?" the landlord asks you, shining the flashlight on a long, thin crack emanating from the rear of the home in a jagged line, extending about halfway across the wall in a lightning-shape. You don't know. You never took an inventory of cracks in the foundation.

"I don't know," you say.

"Hmmm," he says, shining the flashlight around some more. "Well we've got to get somebody in here to take a look at this."

Who do you call in such situations? A Seismologist? But someone will come and examine the crack, to determine whether or not the house might collapse. The landlord owns a number of rental properties in the area, and he's a very nice man.

"I don't think you should stay here," he says.

"Okay."

"I mean, I think it's probably fine, but I won't know for sure until I get somebody in here."

"How long will that take?"

"Well," he sighs. "The insurance company says I gotta get a building inspector and an engineer to come and say it's safe, and I can't get them both here until next month."

"Next month?!"

"I know; it's crazy. I called as soon as it happened, but everyone's booked solid. Act of God and all. But I'm worried about the foundation. Gotta make sure the foundation's all right."

"Well...what are we going to do?"

"I got you a room up at that Marriott on Duke Street," he says. "Just a few blocks from here—it's one of those extended stay places, got a little kitchenette and everything. You can come and go, get things if you need to. But I don't think it's safe, what with your wife expecting and all."

"That's...well, that's really nice of you."

"Well, we got insurance. I might have to apply your rent check towards it though. Hate to ask you to share that burden, and I'll get it back to you if I get reimbursed, but right now I think it's the best option for everyone."

"Okay."

He flips his flashlight off and suddenly you're standing in the pitch-black cellar.

"Sorry," he says in the dark.

*

The house is a mess. The bookshelves and hutch fell over;

there are books and broken china everywhere. The nice plates you got for your wedding, the ones you used once a year. The pictures fell off the walls and the glass cracked. Bric-a-brac and knick-knacks strewn all over the place. You hop over a pile of debris and realize that your home is in no condition to accept a child. Apart from the possibility of being structurally unsound, you have done absolutely nothing to babyproof the place. You see death everywhere. Naked electrical sockets waiting for curious little fingers. Sharp table edges and dresser corners. Easily accessible cabinets full of poison, knives, and bleach. Upstairs, the office that will soon be the nursery is literally destroyed.

You sigh, pick up a single book in some stupid effort to clean up. There's nowhere to put it.

"What did he say?" Liesl asks. She's been resting in your bedroom, also a mess, but spared the worst.

"We have to go to a hotel," you sigh. "We've got a room at the Marriott."

"For how long?"

"A month. Maybe longer if they have to do something."

"Well," she sighs, looking around. "Actually, it might not be so bad. We don't have to clean."

"That's true."

"Can we get back in here?"

"Yes."

"Then we can clean up and get the nursery ready."

You nod; you try to think about where to start.

"We're so unprepared," you say.

"It's actually kind of amazing how unprepared we are," Liesl says.

PART FIVE

DON'T WORRY

On Thursday you pick up Hector Siffuentes from the airport. Despite being called to Sri Lanka, Siffuentes reconsidered when faced with the prospect of a lawsuit. His assistant Nadia has informed you that he is not pleased with being threatened, but that he will honor his obligation.

Your obligation is to make sure his hotel rooms are set and then pick Hector Siffuentes up at the airport because you can no longer afford the car service. And so, on Thursday morning, you are frantically cleaning your Volkswagen Golf of coffee cups and errant snack crackers you have consumed on various occasions. You have not cleaned your car in some time. Due to the Earthquake, you are living in a Courtyard Marriott, which makes the cleaning somewhat easier, as there's a giant dumpster in the parking lot. You wonder what future anthropologists discovering your unkempt automobile might discern about your lifestyle. You are clearly unhealthy, over-caffeinated, perhaps hypertensive and diabetic. There are stubborn Jujyfruit smashed into the carpet, which you are scraping off with a plastic knife you discovered. How fortuitous. Crumbs everywhere. It looks like a hoarder owns the car.

You're filling up a trash bag when your phone rings. It's Liesl. It's strange for Liesl to be calling you in the morning. She's usually teaching.

"Liesl?" you ask. "Is everything okay?"

"Something doesn't feel right," she says.

"What doesn't feel right?"

"I don't know, I know what they said, I know they said everything was okay, but I can't feel her moving."

"Okay."

"Do you think the Earthquake could've...do you think it was—I mean, do you think I was stressed out and..."

"No, no no," you say, looking at your watch. "Do you want to go back to the OB?"

"I'm just freaking out," she says. "I just need you to tell me it's okay."

"It's okay."

"You don't think I should go, right?"

"Uhhh..." you say, nervous about the time. "I don't know, is it...if you're not feeling right, you should go."

"I'm fine," she sighs. "I'm fine. It's nothing. I'm just being paranoid."

"You're not being paranoid," you assure her. "I'm sure you didn't—I mean, you didn't fall down or anything during the Earthquake, right?"

"No, no. I was sitting down. It was fine, I just got stressed out. I think I need to just relax. I'll go after school."

"Are you sure? I can meet you at the doctor's, or..."

"No. You're busy—maybe I'm just trying to get out of lockdown."

"What's lockdown?"

"It's this stupid training session today. It's mandatory for all teachers. We find out what to do if there's a gunman in the school."

"What?"

"You know, like during a mass shooting. They show you how to barricade the door, who to call, what to say to the kids."

"They're training you how to barricade the door?"

"I know, right? What am I gonna do? Actually, there aren't even any doors in the learning cottage anyway. It's a trailer. They don't even have doors on the classrooms. So I have to go to the main building where they have doors so I can pretend I have a door to barricade in case some crazy asshole wants to shoot me."

"Just don't go."

"We have to sign this thing though saying we got the training. The principal's all up in our grill about it."

"Don't go. Go to the doctor's. I can meet you there."

"Don't you have to pick up that guy from the airport?"

"Yeah, but...I should be done by one—I can shoot over there after. I mean, I can get there later."

"You don't have to meet me. I'm a big girl."

You look at your watch.

"I'm just being paranoid, right?" she asks.

"I'm sure it's nothing," you say. "Don't worry."

*

You want to make sure everything's set with Hector Siffuentes's two suites at the Ritz Carlton. You plan to check in for him. You pull in the turnaround and a bellhop greets you with a silver tray of cookies. Andrew Jackson's cookies!

At the front desk, a perky receptionist welcomes you to the Ritz Carlton.

"How may I assist you?" she asks.

"Yes, I'm from Quill & Pad? I had two suites reserved under Siffuentes?"

"All right, Mr. Siffuentes, just give me one moment," she says, typing. You see her nod, and then look nervously at an older man helping someone else.

"I'm sorry, sir, can you wait just one moment?"

"Is there a problem?"

"I just need to check something with my supervisor," she smiles. You see the older man hand a guest keycards, and then your agent whispers something in his ear. He nods, he looks at you, and then he smiles and walks over to you.

"Are you John?" he asks.

"Yes. Is there a problem?"

"No, no, we just have a note to contact Sandi when you arrive," he says, taking up where your agent left off. "She'll be right down. Your guests will be with us three nights?"

"That's right."

"We have their suites all prepared, don't worry, I know Sandi just wanted to greet you personally."

"Uh, okay, will this take too long? I hate to ask, I just...I have to be at the airport in an hour..."

"Here she is now," he says, nodding behind you. You see Sandi walking towards you. She looks like a runway model. She smiles and extends her hand while she's still ten feet away.

"John," she says. "Great to see you. We're so thrilled to have Quill & Pad here again."

"Thank you," you say. "Just, uh...thanks, Sandi."

"No problem, I wonder if we could step over here just a moment?" she asks, motioning behind the desk.

Uh oh.

You walk behind the desk with her to an office, and she closes the door behind her.

"Is everything all right?" you ask.

"Well, you remember how we asked for that deposit?" she asks. "You and I went back and forth on it?"

"Yes, of course. The $25,000. I couriered the check last week…"

"We got the check, but I guess accounting said it didn't clear?"

"No, that can't be," you insist, although you're not entirely surprised by this. You were hoping they wouldn't cash the check until after the benefit.

"*Yeaaah*, look, I know you said you collect a lot of your money at the event, but, the thing is, my hands are a little tied here. I guess last year it took them a long time to get the payment issue resolved, and, well…we did discount the deposit, based on our long history, but I've really done all I can on my end…"

"Wait. What do you mean?"

"Well, this isn't going to affect your event, I know we're upon it now, but…we just…for the suites, I think we're going to require an alternate form of payment. Do you have a company credit card, or…?"

"This can't be right," you say, with a flare of pique. But you are quite aware that you now have a problem. "There must be some mistake."

"Well, if you just have a company credit card…"

Company credit card! Ha ha!

"I don't have the company credit card on me," you say.

"Well I'm afraid, it's just…they're not going to release the rooms without a guaranteed form of payment. I'm sorry," she says.

You sigh, you shut your eyes tight. This is how it begins.

"Fine," you say, and you hand her your personal credit card. She looks at it for a moment.

"Is this your personal credit card?" she asks.

"Yes."

"Um. John. You do realize these suites are $3,200 a night?"

You nod.

"And with room and tax that's going to be more than $20,000?"

"Well, I don't know what else to do," you say. "I have to get them into these suites. They're going to be here in half an hour."

She taps the card against her hand, gives it back to you, and then nods, motioning you back to the desk.

"Are we all set?" the older man says.

"We're fine, Alex," she says, patting his lapel flirtatiously. "Don't worry. Quill & Pad has been with us for forty years. I'll vouch for them."

"Sandi, it's uh, it's the system...I can't...it won't let me..." Alex starts.

"I said they're good for it," she says strongly, typing something in the system. "And if there's any problem, you can bill our department, and events will take care of it."

Then she winks at you, hands you a set of keys, and directs you to the twentieth floor.

"Thank you," you say, and your heart sinks as suddenly you realize that this is this poor woman's *job* on the line. She just vouched for you, and you're not going to pay her. You have no intention of paying her. In the end, they're going to eat that twenty-thousand bucks, and that's just the start. And poor Sandi? Well, she's going to find out what happens to you when you do something nice for people. When you ignore hotel policy, which is there for a damn good reason: to keep swindlers like you from dicking them over.

*

The adjoining suites on the twentieth floor are worth $3,200 a night. Plus tax. Each suite is a two-bedroom apartment, with a full kitchen, three bathrooms, and a living room. You've reserved 8,000 square feet of space at the Ritz Carlton in Washington DC, for this asshole and his ghost. This guy makes his living giving campus readings for $500 a pop. He's probably lucky to get an economy room at the Motel Six in Champaign, Illinois.

There's a plate of chocolate-covered strawberries in each suite, along with a bottle of white wine. The strawberries and wine are welcome amenities from Sandi and the staff at the Ritz Carlton. They are not free. Each amenity is $175, plus room tax and gratuity.

You're not hungry. But you eat those fucking strawberries anyway. You eat them until you feel sick.

*

The cell phone lot is full, so you have to drive around the circle five times. You can't wait more than two minutes or the police will threaten to impound your car. Terrorism and all. The flight's delayed, which is really screwing up your plan to meet Liesl at the OB's office. You keep getting text alerts about the flight status. They all say the same thing: the flight's delayed, and they will text you with further updates.

You are thinking about what to say at your board meeting tomorrow morning. At that meeting, you will deliver a detailed plan laying out the actual practical steps of bankruptcy. You have collected almost all your donations for the benefit, but by weekend's end you will no longer have enough money to continue operations.

The first thing that will happen is that you will stop being paid. Your health insurance will cease at the end of the month.

Thankfully, Liesl's insurance will take over, but after the baby arrives, there will be no money for the duration of her maternity leave. At six weeks, she will return to work, and you will evidently stay home with your daughter having burned through your entire savings, which were already burnt through the last time you lost your job.

You will pack what you can store and vacate Quill & Pad's office, which the organization has occupied for the last four decades. Photos of the most famous men and women in American letters hang on the walls, taken before the advent of digital technology. They are unique artifacts. There is T.S. Eliot laughing at Truman Capote. There is Norman Mailer being interviewed by George Plimpton. There is Eudora Welty in conversation with Kurt Vonnegut, with Robert McNamara nursing a scotch in the background. All the writers in formal wear, mingling with the guests of the Quill & Pad Benefit Dinner, attended each year by 600 of the most powerful people in Washington. Presidents, senators, judges, and journalists appear on the Sunday morning talk shows to eviscerate each other, but on Saturday nights they mingle and gossip with one another on the Washington Benefit Circuit. They will not miss Quill & Pad. They barely even know they are attending Quill & Pad.

Saturday, it will be no different. On Saturday, you will host that same black-tie dinner. And on Monday, you will begin to unravel Quill & Pad brick by brick. You will receive your bill from the Ritz Carlton, which itself will exceed your remaining cash on hand. You will stiff the Ritz Carlton, and then you will stiff Kathy Apple, and then you will stiff the caterer, your landlord, and everyone else the organization owes money to. Starting with its accounting firm.

Your phone buzzes.

The flight is delayed. We will text you with further updates.

You turn on the radio. A man is being interviewed about robots. He is a distinguished professor at MIT and has authored a book that explains the implications of exponential technological progress.

"By 2040, we will have reverse-engineered the brain. We will understand the chemical reactions and storage functions involved in the shaping of human memory and emotion. Basically, we will understand how to manipulate the fundamental building blocks of human experience. Based on current logarithmic trajectories, the raw computing power available in 2040 will vastly exceed the sum of all human intelligence. At this point, what we think of as 'artificial intelligence' will be beyond our comprehension unless we merge with machines."

"What do mean when you say it will be beyond our comprehension?"

"At a certain point, we will not be able to distinguish between human intelligence and artificial intelligence. They will become one and the same. It's quite a difficult concept to grasp, actually, but think of your cell phone right now, and the tools at your disposal, today, right in your pocket. Instant communication with anyone in the world. Access to all the information ever collected in the history of mankind, in a device no larger than a deck of cards. Just twenty-five years ago, that device you take for granted would've seemed like science fiction. In today's world, it's increasingly difficult to function without it. But when you really stop and think about it, the actual 'smart-phone' interface is absurdly primitive. For one thing, it's slow. You have to type all these commands in, or press buttons, which limits how small the device can get. And you still need to filter your search somehow, and we do that now in these big long lists you have to scroll through. All that will be done for you, and you will have an implant right in your brain. You'll be able to think of a question and it will be answered instantaneously and accurately, and not only that; you will possess that information like you control any human memory. It will be as if you always knew it, and that information will interact with your other memories and inform your experience. And if you want to speak with someone, you will simply think of that individual, and you will be able to interact with that person directly through the implant, no matter where you both are physically."

"Like...telepathy?" the interviewer asks incredulously.

"In a way, yes, because we're not simply talking about a telephone call you make in your brain. I'm describing an exchange between consciousnesses. You will feel what the other person feels, see what they see. And what does this mean for our concept of individualism? You see these debates about identity just beginning today, surrounding platforms like Facebook and Second Life, and we talk about our 'Virtual Identity,' and our 'Actual Identity,' but by 2040, there will be no distinction. And it will simply become necessary to augment our brains with computers just to understand what is happening around us, as self-replicating, self-improving machines will actually increase the rate of technological change. And quite dramatically, I might add. Technological advances are exponential by nature, not linear. So think of how fast things are changing right now, and then imagine the world changing one-hundred or one-thousand or ten-thousand times faster than that. And that rate of change will simply keep increasing. What will seem impossible in the morning will be possible by afternoon and obsolete by the end of the day, and we will have the ability to manufacture these innovations so cheaply and so immediately that we will constantly be upgrading ourselves. It will replace traditional education. Those that cannot or will not augment themselves will be left behind, and very quickly they will literally not be able to interact with the world. Imagine them as isolated, primitive, hunter-gatherers stranded on a remote island, and they are occasionally visited by beings centuries or even millennia ahead of them technologically. The non-augmented will see the advanced class as gods. And they *will* be gods, in many respects. Immortality will become a functional reality, as we will be able to download our memories and share them with one another instantaneously, just by thinking about it, or store them, or place them into an android with no discernable difference from human beings. We will be able to store our entire consciousness inside a space no larger than a paper clip, and that consciousness will be instantly accessible to anyone, through the air, directly from your implanted neural interface."

In 2040, your daughter will not even be thirty-years-old.

You should really keep smoking.

*

You make it to the OB's office fifteen minutes late. Liesl's already on a reclining table in an examination room. She's wearing an ultrasound belt around her belly and she's covered with white stickers attached by wires to machines.

"They're just monitoring me," she assures you.

"You skipped lockdown," you say, setting your coat down.

"I'm just being paranoid," she says.

The doctor comes in reading a chart.

"Well, Liesl, let's take a look here," the doctor says.

"I'm crazy," Liesl says.

"No no, always best to be on the safe side," the doctor says. But you can tell she's thinking, *didn't we just go through this?* "Basically, I'm gonna tell you what I told you last week, Liesl; everything looks fine. The baby looks fine. I am still a little concerned about your blood pressure, but it hasn't gotten any worse. It's normal to be a little elevated. It's actually a little better than the last time we saw you."

"So everything's fine?"

"Everybody's fine," she says, and then she swats Liesl's arm lightly with her chart. "Listen, I know this is your first, but you're not due for almost two months. You can't spend all that time worrying. The worrying itself is the problem. So try not to worry so much!"

RECKONING

In the morning you have the board meeting, and then some dead time before the welcome dinner for Hector Siffuentes. The board meeting is held in Albert's imposing boardroom on the tenth floor of his building. It's a huge, cavernous room with twenty-foot floor-to-ceiling glass windows looking out on K Street, the heart of Washington power. An enormous, white marble conference table nearly forty feet long stretches the length of the room. The table itself is a marvel. It must've been installed when the building was built, because it appears to be one seamless block. As you're distributing copies of your bankruptcy plan around the table, you look for the break in the marble, but there is none to be found. The table is like an ancient Egyptian mystery to you. You imagine that it must've been hoisted by cranes through the open windows at some point in the distant past. But where was it quarried? How was it transported?

You have arrived ninety minutes early to set up and rehearse your presentation. Albert's Administrative Assistant Cindy is there, too, making sure the catering is set. The catering is quite elaborate, with coffee, pastries, fruit, several types of tea, soft drinks, and bottled water. There's enough food to feed fifty people, and feed them very well.

"Do you think there's enough?" Cindy asks.

You are wearing your best suit. Your best suit cost $350 at Macy's, and you have owned it for three years. This is the suit you will interview in. It is the suit you will wear when you are questioned by creditors and lawyers. The irony of the opulence and abundance around you doesn't escape you. Alice Cavanuagh-Williams has made it clear that she will not give any more money to the organization while you remain at the helm. Algernon Albert has contributed about half the organization's total budget this year, and he hasn't offered to give any more. You cut your staff; you cut your own pay (and didn't tell your wife about it). You've raised what you can from foundations, from corporations; and from the benefit, you cut everything you could, but in the end, it was simply not enough. You're almost $300,000 short of the million you needed, and that was simply to keep the financial charade of Quill & Pad going. If you had raised that last $300,000, all that would've happened was that you would need to raise another new million next year. All you were trying to do was forestall the discovery of years of mismanagement and neglect. You were building a house of cards in a windy room, just sustaining the lie a few more months, so you could get a full fiscal year under your belt and move on, and leave the problem for someone else to inherit.

And you couldn't even do that.

You've failed.

Again.

So why do you feel so serene as you rehearse your talking points? Wasn't there something more you could've done? Sure there was. But you cannot imagine what it might've been. You could've stopped paying yourself altogether, but even that would've been an empty gesture. The difference between $300,000 short and $250,000 short is no difference at all in terms of practical outcomes. Bills would still not be paid. People would still ask questions. And God knows you worked for it. You don't feel guilty about it. Maybe you should.

It doesn't matter now.

*

"How could you let us get to this point?" Alice Cavanaugh-Williams spits furiously, flipping through your report. "How could this happen?"

"As I said in our previous meetings—"

"I had no idea things were this bad," Alice says, tossing the report back on the table. "No idea."

"I..."

"Alice, it's not like he didn't tell us," Jess Abernathy says.

"Well maybe he told *you*," Alice spits. "This is an embarrassment. An embarrassment."

"He's been telling us for months!" Jess says. "What did you think was gonna happen?"

"I thought he would find the money. Isn't that what we pay him to do?! I'm sorry, but this is just...this is criminal. It's criminal. This is criminal negligence is what this is."

"Alice..."

"Three-hundred-thousand dollars? Do you all think *I'm* going to write that check? Because I'm not. I am done. I have poured my blood, sweat and tears—and no small amount of money—into ensuring this organization's success. For years. Years. Decades. And I'm sorry, but I don't see any of you filling those seats tomorrow night. *I'm* the one twisting arms. I'm the one making phone calls and making the seating charts—do you have any idea how difficult it is to find people to come to this benefit? They don't come for the writer. They don't come for Quill & Pad. They come for *me*."

"You know I hate to correct a lady," Algernon says from the head of the table. "But they don't come for you, Alice. They have never come for you. They come for me. And they've always come for me."

An uncomfortable silence fills the board room, and Alice looks stunned.

"Well…I'm not talking about *you*, Algernon…"

"Yes you are talking about me, goddamn it!" Algernon shouts, slamming his fist on the table.

Everyone in the room turns to face Algernon, who clearly doesn't regret losing his temper. You're more stunned than anyone. He wags his finger in Alice's direction.

"Now, I liked your father, Alice. He was a man who knew the value of things, even if he had the world handed to him on a silver plate; he never asked for anything. He inherited his money, too, but by god that man spent his life earning every penny of it. He had *character*. But I guess you can't inherit *that*, can you? Maybe it skips a generation; I don't know. I'm only here because he asked me to be here. If I never have another one of these goddamned benefits it'll be too soon for me. But I play my part. I always play my part. I write my checks and I buy my seats to everyone's party so once a year they will come to yours. And I show up and sit where you tell me. And there I am, the doddering old fool. And I've kept quiet and let you run your little dog and pony show and feather that woman's nest out of respect for that man's memory, and because I've always felt what goes on behind closed doors is nobody's business. It's unseemly to have to address it in public and I don't care for it."

The room is silent as he leans back in his chair. He lets the silence sit there for a moment, and then smiles.

"Now all that said," he says calmly. "This is your little show, Alice, and it's always been your little show, and I won't stand in the way. If you want to fire this young man, I won't object."

"Thank you, Algernon."

"Provided we live up to our written understanding with him. That's only fair. Wouldn't you agree that's fair, Alice?"

"I..."

"Yes you do," Algernon says, standing slowly. "You agree that's fair, Alice. Now we have a sticky problem. Tonight is our most important evening of the year. It would be untoward to air dirty laundry in front of company. Yes. I think his absence might be noted."

"I don't understand," you say. "Am I fired?"

"I'm sorry, was that confusing?" Algernon asks.

"Sort of?"

"Yes. You're fired," Algernon smiles, as if he's just done you a favor. "So it's entirely up to you. I know we'd all appreciate it if you could manage the introductions. Just for appearance's sake. So we have a smooth evening. Don't you think that would be wise, Alice?"

"What?" she says quietly, staring down at the table.

"I said, don't you think it would be wise to retain Mr. MacManus through the introductions this evening?"

"Yes," she says softly.

"Well, I think he might appreciate being asked nicely," Algernon says. "Alice, will you ask Mr. MacManus nicely?"

Alice looks up at you, and she seems like a very small child to you.

"Will you please stay through the introductions?" she asks you.

"Of course," you say.

"Now you say thank you, Alice," Algernon says.

"Thank you."

"Fine. Good. Please and thank you, that's where we start," Algernon says, and Cindy brings him an envelope. "Now, I've read your agreement personally, and as I understand it, we are obligated for some severance. And as you've displayed such fine character— wouldn't you agree he's displayed fine character, Alice?"

Alice nods.

"Yes, Alice agrees you have displayed fine character. As you've displayed such fine character, I think a little consideration is in order for that as well. But as there's no money left in the coffers, I've taken the liberty of preparing your severance personally."

He carries the envelope down to you and places it in front of you. You don't look inside. You don't need to.

"Thank you," you say quietly.

He squeezes your shoulder and smiles at you.

"Did you get a Danish?" he asks.

BENEFIT

You arrive at the Ritz Carlton at 5:30, ready to meet Hector Siffuentes and escort him to the reception in the Thomas Jefferson ballroom. He does not meet you in the lobby. Perhaps he's forgotten.

You try his cell. He does not pick up.

You try the house phone and dial his room. He does not pick up.

Perhaps he's already at the reception room? You jump on the escalators and check the Thomas Jefferson Ballroom. The bars are set, along with the step-and-repeat with Quill & Pad's logo plastered all over it. The photographer is there checking his camera. But the room is empty.

You try the house phone again, but there's still no answer.

Board members will begin arriving in twenty minutes, and so you jump on an elevator and visit the Presidential Suite. You need a special key to access the floor, and luckily you happen to have one. Actually, you have the spare to the adjacent Ghost's suite, having checked on it to ensure all was in order after purposefully defrauding the Ritz Carlton.

The floor looks like any other floor. It's not the top floor. The carpets are the same. The decorative endtables are the same. The little vases and the little flowers. It's all the same. From the outside, the only difference between the suites and any other normal guest room is that they have double doors, and the fact that they each have a doorbell.

You ring the doorbell to Hector's suite. Nobody answers.

You knock on the door. Nobody answers.

You check your watch. Ten minutes. In ten minutes your board of directors, which has collectively just written checks in excess of $2 million, will be waiting at the reception downstairs to greet Hector Siffuentes, who happens to be huge in the Gay Latino Poetry Community. You are normally a fan of privacy, but in this instance, you feel somewhat responsible for what happens next.

And so you walk to the adjacent suite and slide your key into the lock. Green light. You walk inside the Ghost's room.

"Hello?" you call. "Mr. Siffuentes?"

No response.

"Hello?" you say again, but nobody answers. Now you are walking through the suite. The adjoining door is unlocked and opens into Hector's suite. You walk inside and call out his name again, and still there is no response. But the room certainly looks lived in. The man's been here for twenty-four hours. It looks like he had a party in here the night before. There are several empty wine bottles, an empty bottle of scotch in the small living room, and all manner of snacks and nuts. It smells like cigarette smoke. And there's a woman asleep in a contorted position on the small couch. "Woman" is being generous. She looks like she's about nineteen. She has dyed black hair and several piercings on her face, and she's wearing raggy second-hand clothes. She's covered in an overcoat and she's drooling.

"Hey," you say, shaking her awake.

"Huh?" she says, coming to. She looks at you, confused. "Who are you?" she asks.

"I'm John MacManus. Who are you?" you ask.

"I'm Jamie."

"Hi Jamie. Uh, I'm looking for Hector?"

"What time is it?" she asks.

"Almost six."

"Fuuuuck," she says, sitting up.

"Do you know where Hector is?"

"The poet dude?"

"Yeah. The poet dude."

"That fucker's crazy."

"Yeah. You know where he is?"

"Shit, man, I don't know. They crashed out after I did."

"What happened here?"

"He came to our English class yesterday and then we all went out. After the bars closed we came back here for a drink."

"Is he here?"

She shrugs, lights up a cigarette.

"You can't smoke in here."

"Who the fuck are you, man?"

"You can't smoke in here."

"Oh. Well. Yeah, I don't know where he is, man."

You nod and leave Jamie to her own devices, walking down to the bedroom. Now you're pissed. You knock on the bedroom door but nobody answers, so you open it up, and there is Hector Siffuentes face down atop his $3,200 a night (plus tax!) bed, buck-naked, his head facing the door, his fat ass mooning the ceiling fan, his feet up near the pillows. He's not alone. There's a girl in his bed, although at least she apparently had the good sense to put her head on the pillow and get under the covers. She looks a lot more wholesome than her buddy out on the couch. Also more naked, and more underage.

"Hector," you say, shaking him awake. "Hey! Hector."

He doesn't move, but you know he's alive because he's snoring. The girl wakes up.

"Aaahhh!" she says, pulling the covers up around her. "Oh shit. Oh shit, is he dead?"

"He's snoring," you say, incredulous.

"Oh. Shit. Shit, you scared the shit out of me. Are you a cop?"

"No. I'm…I'm with the hotel."

"Oh. He said it was cool. He said it was cool."

"Don't worry. You're not in trouble," you assure her. "Did he take something?"

"Oh. Shit. Yeah, man, he drank *a lot*."

"Yeah?"

"I mean *a lot a lot*."

You nod, trying to wake Hector up.

"How long has he been like this?"

"I don't know. I guess we crashed around like, noon?"

"How much did he drink?"

"I dunno. A lot. That guy can *drink*."

"But he didn't take anything else? He was just drinking?"

"I'm twenty-one," she says, which is apropos of nothing, and quite difficult to believe.

Suddenly, Hector Siffuentes awakens with a snort, shooting his head up. He looks confused, turning his head to the left and the right. He crawls to his hands and knees, and it's very difficult to avoid getting a glimpse of his flaccid penis poking out from under his huge white gut. He sits on the edge of the bed, as if nobody at all is in the room, and clears his throat again.

"So uh, we've got to go here soon," you tell the girl. "Can you, uh, would you mind getting dressed? And collecting Jamie on your way out?"

"Yeah. Sure, man. Yeah. No problem," she says. You turn back to Hector as she jumps out of bed and runs to the bathroom. Hector has his hands on his knees. Hector is about forty-five years old, but he looks like an old man suffering from dementia. He hasn't yet acknowledged your presence. You're not certain that he knows you're in the room.

"Hector," you say, putting your hand nervously on his shoulder. He looks at you with a start, and you remove your hand quickly. Then he appears to realize where he is. The girl re-enters the room, having hastily dressed, hopping on one foot, pulling a boot on.

"So yeah, cool, it was really cool meeting you, Hector," she says, and she's already out the door, her purse flying like a cape behind her.

He watches her exit and then turns to you.

"Please don't tell anyone," he says. "It would ruin me."

You suddenly realize that Hector Siffuentes is a closet heterosexual. But all you can think about is all the wine bottles you saw on your way in.

"Did you seriously order all that wine from room service?" you ask. "Did you order a bottle of *scotch* from room service?!"

"You can't tell anyone," he says again.

"Do you have any idea how expensive that is?"

"You don't understand...."

"Goddamn it, Hector," you say, shaking your head. "Why did you need the other suite? You can't do this in one suite? Or at a fucking Holiday Inn, for that matter? Do you know how much these rooms cost? All that shit about the Ghost? Why? Why would you do that?"

"No," he says, grabbing your arm, with a terrified look on his face. "You don't understand. You have to believe me! The

Ghost is real! He's real! I swear! I swear it, John! He's here, now, in this room! Laughing! The *future...*the *future, John!*"

By now the board reception's already started, and you really don't care whether Hector is gay, straight, haunted, or not. Some questions you will never answer. But in the next ten minutes, you need this man mingling with some of the richest, most powerful people in the greatest republic in the history of mankind, and then you need him to get on stage and read poems to them.

"I don't really care," you say. "Clean yourself up and let's go."

*

You are here for the Benefit. You have been given a cookie. The cookie has cranberries. The Benefit is for some organization that says it helps kids read. A poet will read poems. A group of delightful black children will read you poems they wrote. During the salad there will be a video of delightful black children overcoming great adversity with the help of the organization. Over dinner a spotlight will locate various teachers around the room. They will speak about the importance of the organization and their important work on behalf of delightful black children. The teachers are strategically placed throughout the cavernous, elegantly-decorated ballroom. You won't listen to them. There are too many of them. They all say the same thing. Tears and commitment and life-changing decisions and what we need now.

It's hard work, but I can't imagine doing anything else.

We can't abandon our children to indifference.

Before the benefit, there are two receptions. You are at the better reception. The reception is for the board and their distinguished guests. The Secretary of Education is there with his *aide de camp.* The Secretary does not wear a suit coat. He wants to look like he is working. He is working. The Secretary hates benefits, but he appears at one every two weeks. He is there to speak at the private reception about the importance of private/public partnerships. He is there to raise money and praise the other side. He is there because one of his boss's bundlers made a gentle suggestion that was not a suggestion.

That bundler is a white-haired, skeletal woman in a metallic dress. She introduces the Secretary in a halting, unrehearsed monotone. The Secretary thanks her and delivers remarks from the podium at the front of the ballroom.

"You know," he says. "I know we disagree on a lot in this town, but this is not a partisan issue. I think we can all agree on education."

Everyone nods.

Education is a partisan issue, and you do not all agree.

At the VIP reception, you are served Beef Wellington and Tuna Tartar by short, Hispanic men in black vests and bow ties, who smile at you and hand you napkins imprinted with the organization's logo and compelling statistics about education in inner cities.

51% of inner city children read below grade average.

47% come from single parent households.

You can make a difference.

The VIP reception is a sea of men in striped blue shirts and yellow ties with strong jaws, emerging jowls, and steely, New England blue eyes. There is no other blue on Earth quite like it. They all look like what you imagine Robert Frost must've looked like. They have homes on the Vineyard. You have never seen them at your Starbucks, your Safeways, your Shell stations. These institutions do not exist in their cities. They live in different cities hiding inside of your cities, in twisted alcoved streets radiating from unknown, northwestern thoroughfares. They live in secret, stately homes located in secret, stately neighborhoods, surrounded by gates and trees. They have a deeper understanding of the world than you do. They are there because of their wives, who chair and serve on various committees for various organizations, who attend each other's various benefits. The men are dragged along to do their civic duty. Everyone writes each other checks. This is how it is done.

There are young wives and old wives, and they are all married to older men. The young wives are stunning. There are a surprising number of brunettes. More than you expected. They are dressed in tight black cocktail dresses, their ample white breasts pushed up in elegant displays of cleavage. They have ridden horses on private estates. Their fathers have owned yachts and sailboats, and their fathers have dutifully sent their daughters to Wellesley and Georgetown and Duke.

The older women are dressed in colorful gowns that ride up to the neck. Their hair looks lacquered, almost like a hairpiece on a Lego figure. Young or old, the women wear enormous jewelry. They have a deeper understanding of the world than you do. They have inherited horses and private estates and yachts. Their fathers' names appear on buildings at Wellesley and Georgetown and Duke.

A photographer is taking pictures of the Benefit Chair, Alice Cavanaugh-Williams, and her guests.

"Oh, John, John," she says, waving you over. "I simply *must* have a picture with John. And where's Kathy? Where's Kathy?"

Kathy Apple steps over, and you stand between the two women, their arms around you. You smile like they do. The photographer takes your picture. Alice Cavanaugh-Williams kisses you on each cheek.

"We simply couldn't have done it without you," she says.

"Excuse me, can I get your name?" the photographer says.

"It's for *Congressional Quarterly*."

"I'm nobody," you mutter.

"Excuse me?"

"John MacManus," you say.

*

There comes a time when you will take the stage to thank the various Corporations and Foundations and Federal Agencies who have supported tonight's events, most of whom you've nearly defrauded, but there's no need to mention that. That's not your problem anymore. You will also acknowledge all the support of your gracious Benefit Chair and all the Board, who have been so supportive. You will thank Kathy Apple. Then you will introduce the poet. You will talk about his stature in the Gay Latino Poetry Community. You will talk about the groundbreaking nature of his work. You will look out on a sea of individuals in tuxedos and evening gowns, the ones who decide things.

You walk to the podium. Alice Cavanaugh-Williams, already on stage, kisses you on each cheek, as if you are bestest friends forever and ever. The light finds you, and the crowd quiets down.

"Thank you all so much for coming tonight and supporting Quill & Pad," you say. You pull out your cell phone and show it to everyone. "Before we begin, I'd ask you all to please silence your cell phones for the duration of tonight's read..."

Your cell phone buzzes in your hand and lights up, the tone attached to your wife's number.

The crowd laughs, and you laugh, too, playfully glancing at the message: *bby cmng now*

You squint at the message.

"Well sorry about tha—"

Then you look at the phone again.

"Baby coming now," you say into the microphone.

ABRUPTION

At 7:02 on a Friday night in Washington, DC, your wife delivered a baby girl. The baby weighs three pounds, and she currently resides in a plastic box under a heat lamp. There is a breathing tube attached to her nose, and several wires and monitors are affixed to her tiny body. There is a feeding tube inserted in her belly button. It appears as if evil scientists are attempting to bestow superpowers upon her.

You are sitting in a metal chair next to her plastic box in a gown and a haircap. There are other babies around you, and next to each of them sits a parent just like you. Some of them are asleep. Some have been here for days. Weeks. Months. Some of their children will not leave this ward. Your child may not leave this ward.

Your baby was not expected for two more months. Around 6:00 p.m., when you were in the hotel room detoxing Hector Siffuentes, your wife, whom you told not to worry, suffered a placental abruption and began to bleed to death during a meeting of the Yearbook Club. Her placenta detached from the unborn baby, causing the baby to begin suffocating. Over the objection of school officials, an English teacher drove Liesl to the hospital, where your daughter was literally ripped from your wife's womb.

Liesl is all right. She is not all right. She has lost a great deal of blood and is recovering upstairs. She will need a transfusion.

"Oh God, it was so scary," Liesl cries. "It was so scary, John, there was so much blood…"

Liesl cannot leave her bed yet. She cannot see her daughter. She is confined to her bed. Several days from now, they will wheel her downstairs to meet your baby girl. Until then, she needs rest. Fluids. Blood.

"I shouldn't have done Yearbook," she sobs. "It was stress. I did this."

"You didn't do this," you say. "It wasn't Yearbook."

Somebody asks her if she's ever suffered a placental abruption before. Somebody asks her if she has any known allergies. People come and go and ask her questions. She lapses in and out of consciousness. Sometimes nurses come and take her pulse while she sleeps. You are not supposed to stay overnight. You will stay overnight. You will sleep in a chair in Liesl's room. Liesl is sharing a room. The woman in the bed next to Liesl sobs uncontrollably for hours. The little shower curtain separating you both does not spare you.

"Basically it is as if she has just been in a serious car crash," one of the doctors tells you, before elaborating on your daughter's chances of survival. They don't know. They'll know better in the morning. Even better in a couple days. She can't breathe on her own. That's normal. She may need a transfusion. That would not be an optimal outcome. Her immune system is not developed yet. A transfusion would be very dangerous. But let's wait and see. Her heart rate is strong. She is jaundiced. That is normal. You cannot touch her or feed her. She may have suffered hypoxia, but we don't know yet. Hypoxia is when the brain is deprived of oxygen. That would not be an optimal outcome. But let's wait and see.

Everybody talks to you for a long time to tell you they don't know a goddamned thing.

We need to be patient. We need to hope for the best.

ASSEMBLY

You stand in the ruins of your home office. Your desk has tipped over and there are papers strewn on the floor. There's so much paper. Old bills, insurance documents, things you need to get to someday, someday. One of the bookshelves has fallen over and dumped its contents everywhere. Why did you keep a jar of pennies on the bookshelf? You gather the papers. You pack the books into boxes. And hour-by-hour, you clear it out until the room is empty, hauling everything down to the basement. When you can't manage to disassemble the bookshelves with a screwdriver, you simply smash them with a hammer and haul the wood outside to the trash.

It's 9:00 p.m. by the time you're finished. You're sweating and exhausted. You haven't slept in two days, but there's more to be done. More. You have to assemble the crib. You must accomplish at least this much. It has come in a giant package from UPS, and it's been sitting downstairs for a month. It weighs a ton. You spent real money on a real wood crib. You wanted it to be nice. There were emails from Babycenter and advisories on toxic cribs from China. No concerns of that here. Now you wish you would've bought the cheap aluminum one, as you drag the box to the stairs, tilt it upright and heave it on the steps. You put your shoulder behind the box and slide it up, trying to keep it from falling over as you push. At the top of the landing you spin it around and slide it into the empty nursery.

You take the box apart with a kitchen knife. The pieces of the crib lie swaddled in foamy protective wrap. They are marked with stickers showing letters. Inside are all the tools you will need to assemble the crib. An Alan wrench, several screws of differing lengths, and an instruction book. The instruction book has no words. Instead, it shows you the pieces of the crib, the corresponding parts with letters, steps 1 through 7. There are arrows and pictures of screws. You are not a particularly handy man, but there are some directions even you can follow.

The light in the room is awful, and so you drag a floorlamp from the bedroom in. You'll need something else later. There's mercury in the bulbs, and if they should shatter, it could poison her. But it will do for now. Outside you can hear crickets chirping. This room has always had bad ventilation. It gets hot in here.

You screw the pieces together, at times having to lay it on its side to get the leverage you need. When you are finished, you get the mattress and the new sheets, the hypoallergenic ones you still need to wash. But you want to see how it looks. You put the mattress inside the crib and put down the dustcover, the pillowed mattress protector, and then the sheet. The sheet is covered with purple elephants. The elephants have tiny jammies on—little pants, sweaters, and little hats. The elephants are all sleeping.

You're in your suit pants and your undershirt, which you've been wearing for three days, and you're wet with sweat. You could use a shower. Before that, you open the window and let the warm August air fill the room. God, it's hot in here. Washington doesn't cool off at night.

You step up to the crib and look down inside. It's only 11:00 p.m. Maybe you can assemble the mobile, too. That would be a real accomplishment. Before you do, you lean over and put your palm on the mattress. You push down as hard as you can, testing the crib's strength, half-expecting it to fall to pieces.

It holds your weight.

Painting by Paul Rutz

Matt Burriesci is the author of *Dead White Guys: A Father, His Daughter, and the Great Books of the Western World* (Viva Editions, 2015), and his stories have appeared in numerous literary magazines. He has served as Executive Director for both the Association of Writers and Writing Programs (AWP) and the PEN/Faulkner Foundation.